8 Stories

By Triece Bartlett

Artwork by Haley Bartlett

The Words

To "Bust Out Stories", who believed in my shorts and encouraged me to keep writing. To the BART boys (Jason and Jay), who read some words and liked them (mostly G.R.). To Evelyn - for inspiring MNDS - I'm still trying to write your posthumous story. To Kate, for her insight at three to know the essence of God and inspire "Occam's Razor." To Haley, for being the superhero Daddy needed. To JJ, AJ, GU for inspiring "Blowing Kisses." The rest came from the ethereal plane, so I must thank God. "Ghost Rabbit" is the most recent of the stories along with "Even Superheroes Need Breakfast." The others were written in the 1990's, for the most part, before rampant cell phone use, September 11th and the horrendous random and purposeful shootings and bombings that seem to have become part of our world and daily lives. Bullying of every sort seems to be part of the fabric of our world. School children can no longer go to school and know they will be protected against the bullies unless they get on the national news or kill themselves. Still, nothing changes. If school children cannot be safe at school, how is the rest of the world supposed to feel safe going to the mall, or a baseball game, or a marathon, or a wedding? I wrote "Chocolate Days" about such things a long time ago. I did not think they would become such common occurrences. As in my poem (in "18 Poems") about Sandy Hook, "Make the world better than this…"

I hope you enjoy the stories, and find some beauty, truth, and love in the words, and between the words.

Ghost Rabbit

Lethargy and a license to kill. He had both. Not willed. Not skilled. Just a Natural. Just lucky. The back woods hunter, who wasn't hungry, but was just shooting at living creatures for sport, and to ease his boredom from time to time. He liked that analogy. He had never seen the backwoods in his twenty-nine years of life.

He turned and looked at the woman lying next to him. Some girl he had picked up on the street. He ran his fingers through his blonde hair and rolled over to grab the pack of cigarettes and silver lighter resting on the bedside table. He propped himself up on the headboard of the hotel room revealing his firm chest and the small bird tattoo on his left shoulder. He lit his cigarette; then blew out some gray smoke in an ethereal exhale. The brunette, in his bed, murmured a humming song then rolled over. The bird on his shoulder (two arched wings) was reminiscent of the first birds children draw. Seagulls by the ocean. He called his tattoo, Jonathon. Many of the people he associated with, lately, didn't get the reference, but he didn't care. It was his secret. He liked secrets.

The girl was hanging on too long. He didn't feel like doing anything, but, he didn't want to be there when she woke up. He thought it was rude of her to be hanging around so long. After all, this was his hotel room. He decided to pull out, pay the bill, and find another hole to dwell in for awhile. He should find some inspiration; some reason to go home; some energy or thought that might let those who thought him missing or dead know he was actually thriving without purpose all these years, but he wasn't ready for that confrontation.

He had made a lot of money doing legal and illegal activities, and spent very little. He had found a way to get many things for free. He had The Charm. Though the life he had decided to live the past ten years had caused some rough edges, his charm was still as strong as ever. He had gotten the job at the "oh so" secret government agency early on in his escape and search for freedom from the easy mundane life he had experienced his first 19 years of life: suburbia, mowed lawns, white fences, the Jones's, the Uppercrust, the right side of the tracks, the Privileged, the evening news, and the way life was supposed to be for everyone, but he just liked to call it the Lie or the Brainwash.

When he left that life, he didn't know about the Lie and Brainwash, he just knew about the boredom, and that there had to be something more akin to the dramas on T.V. The real grit of life. He laughed at his own naive ideas of the world. He thought he was so smart at 19, and, in some ways, he was, but in other ways, he was just part of the joke.

He finished his cigarette, rolled out of bed, threw on some dark and nondescript clothes, grabbed his duffle bag, and walked out of the room. The room was paid through tomorrow. He told the guy at the door to kick the chick out whenever, but to let her sleep for a while. "Send up some breakfast in bed in an hour or two. Tell her she can stay through until tomorrow…the room is paid. Whatever." The doorman smiled at him like he knew him, but nobody did.

The underbelly of life called him by many names. When he first started working for The Agency, his innocent "boy-next-door" good looks and charm gave him the "Boy" nickname. "Send in the "Boy."" As he gained experience, he did not lose his boyish charm and looks, but his nickname changed to "Rabbit." Short for Rabbit's Foot. No matter what the mission was, or what the stink was, his cover was never blown, and as things exploded around him, he walked out, untouched. As time went by, most of the people he worked with retired, one way or another. He was so good at what he did; they kept him a secret from any new employees. He became known as the "Ghost." Basically, he could kill anyone he wanted or was told to kill.   It didn't make any difference. He was covered. He never was caught, but if he ever had been caught, one phone call would have wiped everything clean, as if he never existed.

He walked down the gray streets of the city, not caring which one it was. Everything was gray: the ground, the buildings, the sky, and the other people walking down the street this time of morning. The wind was blowing a chill through the air. He didn't feel cold. He felt nothing. He felt tired. Part of an old newspaper blew on top of his shoes, and he kicked it away. He needed to get today's paper and a cup of coffee, but he was on assignment today too. His next assignment would come in today's paper. He had done a job for a gang leader a few days before, just for fun. It had been all over the news, so he had decided to lay low for a few days before completing The Agency job.

He walked into the coffee shop with its marble countertops and checkerboard floors. He checked the cork board for any sign of movement, but there wasn't anything there. "Hazelnut Cappuccino, Nutmeg sprinkle, Lemon Raspberry Scone. Ten dollars. What? Are you adding a tip in or something? The price of everything. Yeah, oh…and today's paper." "Save two bucks and see if there's still one on the round table next to the far wall." The barista pointed. He grabbed his cappuccino, scone, and a napkin then headed towards the far wall. Above the table, there was a painting from a local artist, "Sarah Pee." A bunch of pink and purple swirls with glittery silver highlight swirls. If he looked really hard, he could see the shadow of a naked woman sitting on her legs and throwing her head back in laughter. There was a window next to the table. He could see the street from here and wait for his target. He straddled the small round chair with the high wood swirled back of diminishing heart shapes. He started sipping his cappuccino, eating his scone, and searching the paper for clues to his next assignment: page five, "Who's Dead Weight on

4

the Board of CompCo." Five sentences in, the list is revealed. One name is spelled incorrectly. That is his next target. His last target. He looks at the Classifieds. There is an ad for a job. "Ghost: Hunter: Retired: Need New Playmate." There is the P.O. Box where he had sent his resume to The Agency. "Start the 5th." They had accepted his resignation, and he would complete the "5" job, and walk away. He had heard stories about The Agency eliminating past agents, instead of letting them retire. He heard the last job was always a set up for the agent.

His current target was in sight. He picked up the paper, rolled it under his arm, and walked outside as the target walked through the doors. The newspaper was at the right level for a heart shot, and the doors were right for people coming in and out at the same time to be close enough to pull off the shot. The silencer made everything a mystery. He walked down the street and didn't look back, but he knew what had happened. The target had walked a few steps inside with a smile, then turned white, grabbed its chest, then crumpled to the floor. There was no blood. The gun was a micro gun. It only shot particles tiny enough to go through the targets clothes and hit the target in the chest: digitalis, insulin, or any other drug that followed the "health issues" of the target that would cause overdose and heart failure or some other failure within seconds or days. The drug would dissipate without a trace or would be a drug they were already taking, and look like an accidental overdose of a drug already ingested: natural causes. The Agency had come a long way since he had started with them. The job was much cleaner now, but still, sometimes, the old fashioned way was best. Sometimes, a message had to be sent. Sometimes, there was more than one target. Sometimes, things needed to be loud.

He discarded the newspaper, and hailed a cab. "Airport." "Yes, Sir!" "Why is a whitebread driving a cab? Are you Agency or Iraq?" "Both." "Then there must be a bag under the seat for me." "Absolutely!" He grabbed the bag and ran it through some tests first. He opened the bag, and found his paycheck: always cash at drop points, cabs, or wherever he named. Disguises, destroyed personal records, leather, and layers, had kept him alive. Having friends in many places who owed him a favor also helped. Being careful, being the best, and not caring. Slow, lazy, and lucky. He had been challenged a few times, but even when he didn't' know it was coming, he never got caught. No one really knew what he looked like, not even the women. He never paid. He just found one when he wanted one. They always came with him. Sometimes, he just took what he wanted, but usually, he used his charm and talents to get a lady to come back with him. Anywhere.

One woman agent was in the right place. It was after the records were burnt; after he set up the contact system; after everyone at the agency who knew anything about him had retired. He met her after a job when he still felt the power-rush and awesome godlikeness. He

6

had walked into a nearby bar to celebrate and watch. The familiar siren song rang through the streets, the dance of the white, red, and blue lights flashing against the walls of the building, the burning smell in the air, and the screams made him high. Some of the people in the bar ran out into the street to see what was happening. A small local band had stopped playing as the hysteria out on the street crescendoed. A few bar patrons, either too scared or too drunk to care, stayed and paid no attention to his job well done. He liked these people. He felt a kinship with them. He always walked to the bathroom, which was usually the furthest thing from the front door in a bar (no one noticed him coming in as everyone was going out). He checked himself, maybe cleaned up a bit…duffle bag of money might have been left in the John or out back of the bar…he didn't remember. He changed his clothes, walked to the bar, and ordered a Vodka Martini and asked, "Where did everybody go?"

"Man, oh Man…didn't you hear that explosion?"

"I was in the bathroom."

"You still could've heard it."

"I was having my own explosion. Anyone know what happened?"

"Not yet, man. But it looks bad."

He took a sip of his Martini. The bartender was good. He would leave him a great tip.

"Wow, Man!"

"You said it!"

He always tried to pick up on the local lingo. He was good. He had become a Chameleon…

but they still called him Ghost. After a while, neither his enemies nor his allies were sure if he was a man or a woman, but he had played both parts.

The Agency Woman walked up to the bar. "A Cosmo," she said. He wasn't sure about her status, but, whatever. She was hot.

"Do you have any food here?" He asked.

"Just nuts and pretzels, but there are a few restaurants down the street."

"I just really feel like having a burger."

The woman hadn't left after getting her Cosmo. She had been talking to a few other men when he had walked in, but changed her target. She had been staring at him, sipping the Cosmo, and listening. "I'd like a burger too."

"Then you should get one." He said.

"I have a better idea," she said.

"You must be the luckiest guy. You should buy a lotto ticket," said the bartender.

They both finished their drinks, and walked outside together.
"Do you have a place nearby?" He asked.

"No. You?"

"No. Car?"

"No. You?"

"Yes." He said. She seemed surprised, but he was full of surprises. "This is my car." He pointed to a red fuel efficient vehicle. It was typical, nondescript, normal, and average.

"Really?" She asked.

"What were you expecting? Something more expensive? You can beat it then!" He was having fun.

"No. No. Do you live nearby?"

"No. I'm in town visiting family. You know. Family reunion. Today was the last day. Just had to get away from everyone. Mom expecting more and Dad expecting less. Siblings competing. Aunts pinching cheeks and asking when are you going to settle down and have some kids. Aunt Jo coming up with alcoholism so no booze anywhere in sight to numb the numbness or be an excuse for acting badly. Just needed a drink. Dad and Mom decided to be vegetarians, so no meat..."

"...so you wanted a burger."

"You pick up on things quick." He WAS having fun. "Yeah, I told them my flight was a little bit earlier than it really is so I could sneak some fun, real drink and food in before my flight."

"When's your flight?"

"Tomorrow morning."

"Were you going to party all night?"
"I had no plan. I was staying at my folk's house to save on a hotel room, but I thought I could sleep at the airport or get a room for the night, if I needed to, but if you have a place…"

"Oh, no…I just …I live with my parents."
"Wow," he thought, "She really sucks…that is the last resort excuse for an agent…she wasn't prepared." She didn't even look like she lived with her parents. Too metropolitan.

"Oh, and you were judging me on my car…which is the same car I own when I get home! You don't even own a car or have your own apartment! I have my own apartment! Do you even have a job?"
"No. I lost my job last week." "She really did suck, "he thought, but she was hot. Really hot. She wasn't wearing underwear.

She started laughing. "You're right! I came out tonight to forget my life. To meet up with someone to have a good time so I felt beautiful, and rich and perfect. What the hell am I doing?" She was getting better. She even started to cry. He leaned against the rental car, pulled her to him and started kissing her. She fell into him. He opened the car door and drove around until he found a burger joint. They drove through and picked up some food. They ate food in the car while he looked for a seedy motel to take her to.

They made love and made love. She was good…he was good. They were bad. He kept waiting for her to make her move. Nothing. They fell asleep. He didn't really. He waited. She didn't really. She waited.

She got up. Walked to the window, pulled the curtain aside, and looked outside, then took a deep breath. She went to the bathroom. He walked in on her and got the drop on her.

He had checked her for weapons, and found none. He had hoped he was wrong about her, but didn't really care. She had something new, a cell phone that turned into a gun and lipstick that held bullets in the base. He loved The Agency magic. He could have his whole world in a cell phone and travel light.

He dressed in her clothes when he left. They were watching. He left them a message: "Never try this again. I'm better than you'll ever be –and I don't care." He had used her blood and her hand to write the message on the dirty white linoleum of the bathroom floor. He had no finger prints, and his DNA match came up as Abraham Lincoln on any database.

He had found his own technology - outside The Agency. For every Agency, there was an Anti-Agency. He had friends there too. He had friends that were crazy, yet brilliant: hermits, conspiracy theorists, war mongers, and those sweet souls who just wanted peace and spoke to the dead: society outsiders who cared more than he did about the outcome, or the balance, or fairness, or survival, or anything. For him, it wasn't about right or wrong, or even money. His life, after suburbia, was about feeling alive, about having the hardest challenge or target or project presented to him, and accomplishing it – not knowing if he would succeed and not caring – it was the hardest challenge and the success that pushed away the boredom. For a while. He had discovered the lie about his new life. He discovered that he had a talent, but it was too easy. Too much the same. All the faces all looked the same. The truth was – everyone died. He would some day. He wanted to leave more than a legend behind. He loved his freedom. He loved playing the games that changed the world. He loved feeling important and anonymous. He had flown as high as he could, but transcended nothing. Found excitement for a while, but nothing that changed his view of the world. Everything was an illusion, and the people in it were players and pretenders. He hadn't found anything real besides death.

Maybe going back home wasn't the right move, but he had an idea about leaving some DNA behind and doing something less with his time. Maybe, he could live long enough to discover something else that was real.

The whitebread cabby, who was taking him to the airport from the coffee shop, had the same look on his face as The Agency woman and of all of those who had tried to beat him. The airplane flights back home were smooth. The paper he picked up at the last airport had the news of the cocaine overdose of the young taxi driver, who had survived Iraq, but not the Ghost.

His target had been eliminated, along with the gangster twin who had done the fifth job for him. It was always best to die in one life before starting another.

The family reunion was joyful and tearful. Just as he suspected, the High School "Sweet-heart" had married the second best man. Everyone had a right to move on with their dreams if death interrupted them, somehow. Even a fake death. He hadn't thought of her as his number one choice; just the easiest. He was more interested in the smart frumpy brunette girl. She seemed to have a better grasp on what was real than anyone else in High School. He had come back in time for the High School reunion. Hannah was there. The news of his miraculous resurrection was the talk of the town. She was back from a lot of college. She was embarking on a career involving green energy and saving the planet. At first, she seemed to disdain him and most of the class that had ignored and shunned her. She had brought a date, who seemed bought or just braindead. The date fawned over her more than he should, which she seemed to hate. Braindead finally left to go to the bathroom, and left Hannah at the table, alone. He walked over. He didn't pretend or use his charm. He just said, "Hello, Hannah." She said, "Weren't you dead?" He knew she had a great remark to follow, but he cut her off. "Death is the only thing that is real." She stopped; looked up at him; then smiled. She smiled a knowing smile, not the vapid smiles of most of the people who had welcomed him back and patted his shoulder.

His mom had cried and asked him where he had been, then got angry and left a hand print on his face for being alive and not communicating to them.

"Sit down," she said. The date came back, but she shooed him away. "You've been places. Seen things. So, why me?"

"Because the rest of it bores me, and, honestly, I think our DNA would be great together."

"No pretenses? No illusions? What if I want more?"

"I see you with your date. You really want the romance, the love, the vapid fawning fan or someone real to share your life with? Someone who appreciates and respects you?"

"Love is an illusion."

"Doesn't mean we can't work hard, live dreams, laugh, and have fun too. I bet I can make you laugh."

"I bet you can. What's in it for me?"

"Anything you want."

"You raise the kids."

"Sure."

"Do you have any money?"

"Tons."

"Do you care what I'm doing for a living, or care if I work, even if I don't have to for money?"

"No, no, no. I'll support you, but don't ask me to pretend to be excited about your work or job; unless, you can take away the one thing that is real."

"Reanimation, or stop it altogether," she smiled. "That would be my secret passion."

"Now, you might get me to believe in fate, love, or something – because I can't believe you said that."

"Why? Is it your passion too?"

"No, but that it is YOURS, turns me on in ways I haven't felt in a long time."

"How do I know you are not a murderer, or serial killer, or worse?"

"Would it make a difference?"

"Well, I wouldn't want to be next on your list."

"I see your point. How do I know you aren't, or worse?"

"You don't. I don't trust or respect too many people, but I do you. I've watched you pretend and move tonight. You aren't even trying that hard. I don't think you really care about anything or anyone, but I believe this conversation is as honest and as much as you can give or care. Let's see if I have this right: you want to marry me to have some kids to leave some excellent DNA combos behind because you find me stimulating and as real as anything can be without being Death. You don't want or need anything from me besides companionship and kids. Hmmmm. That's the only reason I kept Joe-vapid around. You ARE a much better choice because I find you amusing too. I hate the typical. As proposals go - this is not typical, and intriguing. I would prefer to validate that we are as compatible as we think we are. We should live together for awhile and test daily life interactions, chemistry, and really discover what we hate about each other and see if we can live with that."

"You are such a flirt! How could I say "no" to you?"

She laughed. She had a great laugh.

Two children: a boy and a girl. He saw the world differently through their eyes. He saw something real in them. Everything was new, fascinating, and alive to them. Their discovery was his discovery. He was never bored. She taught him Life was real. In relation, if Death is real, than Life must also be

16

real. Without one, there could not be the other. There WAS a balance. His crazy peace-loving friend from the past was right.

It came on the littlest one's 5th birthday. A warning. He knew what it meant, but she didn't' want to know. A dead seagull on the doorstep. He checked the paper. In the Personals: "Ghost. Found you. Tag. You're it."

He had been retired for ten years. Only a very old playmate who had been allowed to survive retirement could have found him.

The message decoded as: "A Creamy." A meeting was requested at the local ice-cream parlor. The 4th of this month was the meeting date. Tomorrow at 2:00pm.

He walked through brightly colored doors. A grizzled old man with thick gray hair, dressed in khaki shorts, a Hawaiian shirt, and flipflops, was sitting at the bar. The man looked up from his Sundae. Ray. He walked over to him and sat down then ordered a scoop of chocolate chip frozen yogurt. "Shouldn't we both be dead," said Ray. "Yeah. So, do I get a deal or am I just targeted?"

"They may care, but I'm just here to see what can be done."

"How did YOU survive retirement?"

"I was never that important, and I retired with options. Their options. Like now. They can "recall" me or utilize me when they feel like it.

Nothing dangerous. Nothing big. Once a year, I go on a retreat to train new operatives. That usually is the extent. You, on the other hand…"

"Yeah. I know. Dangerous, live wire, important, uncontrollable, wild."

"Yeah. I'm trying to get you an option now. I've been reporting for a few days. They know everything. They're afraid, but I'm trying to convince them you are an irreplaceable asset. We could use a trainer like you on the "retreat.""

"They haven't bought it yet."

"No. They want the random shooting guy walking into the mall when your wife goes shopping with the kids, alone; the drunk driver hitting your parent's car; or we take you out. You or them. I can tell those around you know nothing of your past life."

"A test."

"Yes."

"No escape. If I disappear, all who love me die, but I survive and am free."

"Yes."

"But if I tell them and help them disappear too, they may choose death or never want to see me again anyway."

"True."

"If I allow myself to get tagged, then everyone else goes on, but perhaps, they are testing how much I've changed. They could use the Ghost, not the Family Man. If I sacrifice myself, I'm the Family Man. If I sacrifice everything else, I'm the Ghost. Too bad there isn't a third option since I'm neither the Ghost nor the Family Man," he sighed unconcerned.

"That is what I've tried to tell them."

"Yes. Either way is fine with me. What do they prefer?"

"That you never retired. They fear; yet, need you."

"That is sad," he laughed. Ray joined him.

"So?"

"Let them choose," he said, savoring each bite of his frozen yogurt.

Even Superheroes Need Breakfast

Every superhero needs breakfast. No one can fight the bad guys without feeding their power that makes them special. "Yogurt and a piece of bread, please?"

Flying swiftly around the room with butterfly wings, climbing the tallest buildings, strong, fast, and fierce, with water squirting from under her arms, and fire spewing from the palms of her hands, she saved the little girl that had been kidnapped by the Evil Bat Guy. Her side-kick, Star the Wonder Dog, had a strong bite and fierce bark and flew beside her as they went back home.

The success of each mission was always tenuous. The fight always seemed too close to call, but she always beat the bad guys. She could hear screams for help from miles away and was vigilant at looking through her telescope-spyscope for any signs of trouble, but sometimes, she had to be her mild mannered alter-ego, Haley.

"Clean your place."

She did as she was told, then pretended to be a dragon as she walked up the stairs to brush her teeth. Even superheroes had to brush their teeth! All the superheroes she knew had great smiles.

As she put on her jeans and t-shirt with the image of a popular fairy friend emblazoned on the front, she realized that superheroes needed to know so many things besides how to fight villains and save the day.

Sometimes, there were signs to read: "To the Evil Bat Guy's Lair" or "Help!" Sometimes, you had to read a map, or solve puzzles, or count the bad guys to make sure you got them all.

Superheroes didn't get paid for making good choices and doing good deeds. The alter-ego had to go to school to learn how to fit into the world of the nonsuperhero people.

The alter-ego had to do chores or get a job. Most important was how to tell the good guys from the bad guys. Times tables were important too.

Sometimes, people just needed a smile or a kind word. Sometimes, her friend Sammy would get pushed on the playground, and Haley would stand up to the bully and take Sammy to the office for some ice and a bandage. If someone looked sad or was crying, she always had a shoulder and a hug in her pocket, just in case they needed one.

Then there were days when nothing went right. The days it rained; the leak in the roof and the sniffles. The days none of her friends wanted to play. The days when there was no toast or yogurt for breakfast. The days when Daddy was gone working, and Mommy yelled when the pink juice spilled on the white carpet, and the dog barfed on the floor.

Those were the days the superhero really went to work.

The rain brought rainbows, the leak dripped into a pot that created a lovely pinging rhythm, and the sniffles made the superhero's voice sound like a frog.
If the friends didn't play, Haley played with herself, but there was always someone who needed saving too.

Haley could clean up the dog barf and help clean up the pink juice, and, most importantly, help Mommy laugh again. "Let's play hide n' go seek, bake cookies, dance, sing songs, tell stories, or watch a movie."

Then the very scary days came. The days when Daddy was in the hospital. The first time Haley saw Daddy, he was scary. He looked like the Evil Scar Man. Mommy had told Haley that Daddy's ear was gone and that there was a big scar from his chin up towards his forehead around the bandage where his ear used to be and down the side of his neck curving in a hook on his chest. It was all on Daddy's left side. Even though Mommy told her and also told her to be brave, Haley still found Shock and Fear; her old archenemies. Her eyes got so big. She pierced her lips and tried not to cry, but cried anyway. Her mouth opened in a silent scream as she looked at

Mommy, then ran to her burying her face in Mommy's soft stomach. She didn't want to let go.

Shock, Fear, and Tears came with her on the second day. She was very brave, but didn't want to leave Daddy alone in the hospital.

The third day went the same way, but by the fourth day she was a pro. The Superhero Butterfly Girl put ointment on Daddy's skin graft wound on his leg.

Grandma and Grandpa came too. She slept with Grandma. Grandma took her to school and tumbling and all her Superhero lessons because superheroes never stop learning. Mommy spent a lot of time in the hospital with Daddy.

Mommy and Grandma and Grandpa had talked about cancer and the "C" word. Haley knew what they were talking about. Haley's Grandpa Jack had died from cancer. It was scary.

The doctors had gotten all the "C" word (a squishy Squamish cancer in the parodit gland wrapped around the ear canal).

Daddy had been in pain for months. The first doctor went really slow. Tried to drain it with a needle then it grew fast after that. The first doctor talked a lot, but did little. The second doctor wouldn't see Daddy unless another primary doctor said it was urgent. He was referred to another doctor. That doctor did tests the first doctor did and charged a lot of money, then told Daddy that he would refer him to another doctor for surgery. "No one in this medical group will touch this now...we are sending you to another medical group." . Finally, the fourth doctor, in another group, scheduled surgery-six weeks after the visit-after Daddy waited so long to find a doctor to actually do something. The cyst next o Daddy's ear grew and grew and Daddy hurt. Then the first operation happened. Many of the people – alter egos and superheroes- at home missed Daddy. Daddy so wanted to come home, but two weeks after his eleven hour surgery, he had another three hour surgery to fix the infection and torn apart stitches. Poor Daddy. When could he ever come home? Mommy wanted to sue somebody. The first doctor, mostly.

Mom and Dad were always worried about money. Sometimes, they discussed money loudly. Mommy now talked about the debt, the cost of surgery, and the disability. She talked about losing their home, and the postponement of adopting more children and other fun events. She talked about ending some Superhero classes and moving. Mom talked about getting a job. Mommy had less and less time for the Superhero.

Star, The Wonder Dog couldn't go to the hospital. You would think any Superhero would be welcome in a hospital. So many people in hospitals needed Superheroes.

24

A superhero always saves the day, and does their best to pass every test. Though breakfast and a shower help start the day. Cookies are good too.

Superheroes brighten a room. Even nurses, who help heal, appreciate the songs and drawings of superheroes (especially the drawings on the white board where the nurses would write their names). Doctors tend to rush in and out too fast to appreciate the full effect of a superhero's presence.

But still, whether or not your Grandma and Grandpa are at your house or if your Dad is in the hospital and your Mommy is busy and sleepy, there are so many people who need rescuing. So many cries for help. So many who need saving. So many villains and evil doers. Superheroes need proper nutrition, a strong body, clear thinking, intuitive nature, and logical reasoning. The alter ego must be good enough to protect the Superhero from harm in their non-superhero lives. Superheroes only can marry other Superheroes and they have superhero babies.

"When will Daddy come home?" Not even Haley's superhero powers could hasten his return.

When Daddy did come home, Haley had to use her superhero powers to be quiet, because Daddy needed to rest. She still went to birthday parties, but Grandma and Grandpa went home. She missed them, but would see them soon.

She should've have known that Daddy would be fine. After all, for her to be a superhero, Daddy had to be a superhero too. Mommy had to be a superhero too, but Mommy wasn't feeding her power that made her special. That was the number one superhero rule…feed your power or you will not be able to fight off the Evil Bat Guy or Spider Creepy. There were so many things that could drain your power.

For real superheroes, there wasn't one thing that could drain their power. So many things could take away power. Sometimes, a superhero didn't even know what that thing was, it would just happen. There were several ways to try to build power, but not always the means to build power. Sometimes, one way would not work and the superhero would have to try another.

Haley's blue eye's sparkled with tears as her best friend called her a "fat ass" and another best friend said, "I wish you were dead," and "I hate you." Her powers were draining out her eyes. "Who knew?" She thought.

She told them to stop, but they wouldn't. She tried to ignore them and go someplace else on the playground. She found another friend who patted her on the back and played a game with her, but they followed her and her friend everywhere they went. They couldn't find the yard duty adult. Haley stopped and pushed one of the kids, who cried and ran away. She got part of her power back, but then the yard duty came running, and Haley got in trouble. Her voice tried to tell the adult what had happened, but the adult could not hear her. Her power was gone again.

Mommy had to talk to the adults, but they wouldn't listen or do anything about the bullying. They only took Mommy seriously when she talked about talking to the Superintendent of Schools and a lawyer, but they still did nothing. Mommy talked to the parents of the kids, some of the kids got punished and stopped being mean.

"Why does it take so much for people to listen and believe? Why is it so easy to lose your power?"

Haley met a new boy at school. He came from another school and was older than the rest of the third graders. He seemed to be mean to everyone and punch a different kid in a fight every day. He had been mean to her, but he had also been kind. Haley loved playing kickball. Dorian was the pitcher one day. He rolled the ball too far one way, then too far the other way. Haley barely tapped the ball, and someone said she was out. She went to the back of the line with her head hung low. She felt like crying, but she didn't. Dorian called her back and said she wasn't out. She kicked the ball and made it on base. He had been nice to her. He said she could be his friend if he told on Sarah for doing something wrong, but she wasn't sure. She hadn't liked what Sarah had

27

done to Dorian, but she liked Sarah. Sarah had told the truth, but it was a mean truth, and wasn't necessary to tell. She decided to tell on Sarah. Sarah didn't get in trouble, and Dorian became her friend. Mommy explained that no one is truly your friend if you have to do something or give them something to be their friend. Haley understood, but she knew Dorian needed a friend.

"Dorian is like a Villain on the outside, but on the inside, he is a hero. You know the difference between a Villain and a Superhero? A Villain never has been given the choice or chance to use his powers for good. They were never taught that there are other good uses for their powers. Maybe their Mom and Dad couldn't teach them, or maybe there were no parents, or maybe their parents were Villains too."

Maybe superheroes became villains because the power that made them special was never fed or was fed the wrong way. If you eat the wrong foods, you don't have energy for the day.

That is why superheroes need a good breakfast.

Maybe the difference between superheroes and villains was that villains never got a decent breakfast, and maybe they didn't floss and brush their teeth, so they had cavities that hurt them all the time and put them in a bad mood and made them impatient all the time. Maybe, the only thing that made them feel better was hurting other people. Something like the story about the lion with the thorn in his paw.

Villains might also not feel good about themselves in other ways, so they would have to take things from other people to feel better about themselves. Maybe it is like some rich kids she knew who bought a lot of toys and fancy clothes so they could show off at school. "If you don't have Mondo Puppy Rings, you can't be in our club. I have more Mondo Puppy Rings than anyone, so I'm better than everyone. I'm more special than you because I have Mondo Puppy Rings." Haley knew this wasn't true, but she bought some Mondo Puppy Rings so she could feel like she belonged, and so she could be a part of the club, but the rich kid with all the Mondo Puppy Rings took half of the ones Haley brought to school, then other kids took most of the rest. She gave some away to kids who didn't have any and who couldn't afford to get any. Part of her didn't care if she had Mondo Puppy Rings or if she was in the club. Sometimes, it was hard being a kid and a superhero. There was so much to learn.

Her teacher Catanina taught her about energy and how energy transforms. Dinosaur bones become the fuel for cars. Sunlight helps plants turn carbon dioxide into oxygen. The energy of the sun did many things. Sunshine. She knew two songs with the word "Sunshine" in them. The sunshine bounced off her golden hair and her blue eyes sparkled as she flew on the

29

swing at lunchtime recess. She loved swinging. She could imagine she was flying with her pink butterfly wings to save someone. She also loved gymnastics, but she hadn't been since before summer had begun, and now it was school time again. Mom said they couldn't afford it, and Haley said she would pay with her own money, but her Mom said she didn't have enough. Haley said she would do chores for the neighbors to earn more money to go, but her Mom said she didn't have time for that, and that Haley would not make enough money for gymnastics. Mommy was looking for a job. If Mommy got a job, she wouldn't be around that much anymore, just like Daddy.

Daddy had gone back to work and was away all the time. He was coming home Tuesday night.

She had heard stories about spinning hay into gold, but she knew only people with magic of energy transformation could do things like that. She did not have that power.

Mommy said it was the recession, and Daddy being in the hospital. Haley didn't want to lose her home, so she tried to be super good and help as much as she could, and not ask about gymnastics or more toys or going to Sushi. Besides, she could put those things on her Santa Claus wish list, along with Pillow Animals, Mini-Build-A-Stuffed-Animals, Doll Clothes, and a new bike. Mom said she had to learn how to ride her old bike and take the training wheels off before Santa would bring her a new bike. She also wished for Mom to win the lotto too. And as always, she wished for a brother and sister. She knew they would have to adopt, but there was no time or money for that, and winning the lotto would give Mom and Dad time and money to get a brother and sister. Mom hadn't bought any lotto tickets for some time. She was too busy applying for jobs.

"Yogurt and cinnamon toast, please?" There is no yogurt this morning, nor cereal, nor milk, nor OJ. There is only toast and jam. For lunch, it is the same thing. For dinner, there is rice and cheese and always lots of water. Haley gets up earlier so there is plenty of time to walk to school. She has decided that she loves walking to school with Mommy, and it helps the environment not to drive the car everyday. The car disappears, and there is OJ and cinnamon toast again in the morning.

Mommy and Haley sing a song about a clever magical cat on the way to school and skip.

Telling time is also important. So are new vocabulary words: "perspective."

When Mommy shows up to walk her home, it begins to rain.

When they get home, the fire flickers in the wood stove, and Mommy gives Haley some hot chocolate.

They read books by the fire. Mommy never lets a little rain ruin a perfectly lovely day. Mommy is a wonderful superhero.

Mommy and Haley watch more movies and read more books since the television was disconnected. They also play more together. Mommy has time for Haley since she got a job while Haley is in school at a fast food place. She always shows up at school in her uniform now. Daddy is hardly home. He stays with Grandma and Grandpa mostly. He works all the time. When Daddy comes home; Mommy, Daddy, and Haley's powers seem to grow.

Sometimes, people can be villains without even knowing they are villains. In social studies, Haley learned about different cultures. In some cultures, giving poop can be a gift. Dry poop can be used to burn to stay warm or to fertilize gardens. It may be considered good luck and a prayer for the receiver for warmth and good fortune with their crops or for an abundance of food for their home. The person giving the feces would be considered a generous and kind person, and perhaps, maybe a hero if there was not an abundance of feces for such purposes. But maybe, the house receiving the feces would be embarrassed or jealous that someone else is giving them the poop and feel that this is terrible thing because the superhero seems to be assuming that the receiver can't get their own poop. In other cultures, the poop is an insult. The giver would be considered a villain. All of a sudden instead of hearing, "Thank you for your gracious giving of feces," the superhero hears: "Stop dumping your shit on me!" Even the definition of poop becomes muddied in perspective.

Most superheroes in the stories, at some point, must choose between saving the world, or saving the one they love the most. The Superhero always chooses the world. Superheroes have to be superheroes. It is genetic. Why couldn't another superhero step in and save the one they loved? Or even a regular person find it in their heart to save? Being a superhero and an alter ego, having to pay bills and work a full time job, and then have bad attendance for saving others, and then lose everything and everyone you love because the world needs you, sometimes is too much. Villains use their powers to get what they need to live. They don't have to have alter egos if they don't want to. They use their powers to rob banks. Being a villain looks good. Being a villain looks easier. Though, villains never really win. The good guys always win. And winning isn't everything, but beauty, truth, and love are…and villains never truly have these things.

Haley has these things. Beauty is all around her in everything. Truth is innocence and never changes. Love is Mommy and Daddy, and Star- the Wonder Dog.

These feed Haley's power that make her special…along with a good breakfast, and when Daddy's home, it is always, "WAFFLES!"

4 A.M. Wake Up Call

(*This story was written before cell phones took over the home phone, and pay phones were the main way to call someone without having a home phone.*)

Cherylynn was dreaming about the white ice cream truck. Its tinkling bell music repeating; calling all the children to answer and beg their parents for change for a rocket or a rainbow missile. She ran after the ice cream truck. It had passed her house, and she could not catch up to it, though the tinkling music grew louder.

She reached for her alarm clock to press the snooze bar, but the tinkling and ringing sound continued. She looked at her clock. "Who's calling at 4:00am?" She thought. These early morning calls usually meant some mistake or tragedy had occurred, or someone was drunk and lonely. She reached for the telephone and picked it up in her half awake still dreamy ice cream voice, and said, "Hello." The voice on the other end said, "I love you." Cherylynn responded dreamily still, "Hmmm, that's nice." The phone clicked, and the sound of the dial tone echoed from the receiver. She fell back to sleep.

Her alarm went off at 6:00am. She pressed the snooze bar, but turned off the alarm after her second turn and twist and press of the bar. She arose at 6:30am, showered, and, while she rubbed her head, she wondered if she had dreamt the phone call, or if it had really happened. As she brushed her teeth, she decided it had not been a dream. As she put on her nylons, and slid on her high heeled shoe, she tried to figure out who would call her and say such a thing. She glanced at her watch, ran out her front door, and then drove to work mesmerized by the words, "I love you." She thought about who the articulation could belong to and tried to remember the voice.

She arrived at her job as a receptionist for a reputable law firm. She had been there five years and was content, but still lived in a small apartment alone, with her cat, Sam. As she answered the phone at work, she pondered the vocalization and the mysterious phone call, expecting any minute to hear the voice on the other end of the phone line, saying the same words.

All day long, Cherylynn obsessed about who the caller could be. "My brother? No, the voice is not my brother's. My brother has lived in New England the past ten years and has only called once a year at Christmas. He has also affected a Bostonian tone. My father? NO. It was definitely not my father's voice either." On her memo pad, she listed all the men in her immediate and distant family, and then went down the list analyzing the names and utterances. In the end, she had crossed off all the names. "No. The voice is soft and well meaning. This is not the harsh and cold sound of most of the male members of my family."

She listened closely to her male co-worker's voices all day: her boss as he asked her to type a letter, or take a memo; the UPS man as he dropped off packages; handsome Wells from Accounting, who stopped by to see if she wanted to buy some candy to support his daughter's softball team. None matched the mystical disembodied voice that rang through her head and swirled in her ears.

She thought of her friends; past and present. Anyone she might have the vaguest contact with, but none had the lilting Scottish intonation and the tenor type echoing hum behind the voice; full of emotion and meaning. Three words drove her crazy all day.

"Could it be Bob? He took that trip to Ireland last year. Bob is kind, but gay. No," she thought. "Could it be my friend, Michael, who is always playing practical jokes on everyone in the office? No," she thought. "He wouldn't get up so early for a joke."

"What about my ex-lovers?" She wondered. Sean wasn't beyond the mood, but lacked the meaning. Allen had a deep base voice and could never fake a trembling and passionate tenor voice. Besides, Allen could never say, "I love you." He would say, "Luv ya! Bye-Bye kiddo." Peter had been the one that had really captured her heart. The one that could save her if he could ever get over his fear of falling. He could never say those words, and he could never get that close. He ran every time he saw her. He couldn't pick up the phone to call her and never could fake an accent. "Peter is a coward," Cherylynn thought. There was that one-night-stand, but he was from Texas, and had a very distinguishable accent. No, as much as she tilled her memory to try and drag up a matching intonation, she could not.

"Good afternoon, Finch, Finch, and Addaberry. How may I direct your call?" Cherylynn said as she typed the letters and memos, directed calls, and dreamt about the voice.

"Maybe someone dialed the wrong number? I received the lovely message meant for someone else. Well, didn't that happen to her all the time? Isn't that why she was still single?" She decided that would be the most likely explanation. Someone thought she was someone else, and she got a message intended for someone who may never receive it. "But, the caller didn't identify himself. Wouldn't he want to take credit for the beauty he had created so early in the morning? Maybe he realized his error, and that is why he hung up. He realized that he had called the wrong number. Yes, that was the answer," Cherylynn decided. She preferred to think he was some random thoughtful caller. "Yes. Someone who couldn't sleep and just called any number and said, "I love you," just to be kind and beautiful. He didn't want anything back in return. He just wanted to give something pure and wonderful to brighten a stranger's day." It reminded her of walking down the street and someone returns your smile when they don't have to and don't know you. She like this idea and imagined the mystery caller smiling as she passed him on the street.

Cherylynn stayed late at the office to finish up the letters that were piling up and were so important to go out in the mail the first thing the next morning. She turned out the lights and locked up the office suite and building where she spent most of her time. She never knew what the weather was like outside. She ate lunch at her desk. She arrived when it was dark out, and left when it was dark out. Her car was parked the nearest to the door and the only one left in the parking lot. "I could be a vampire, but I don't think they would spend all day under florescent lights."

She stopped and got gas on her way home. She walked through her apartment door and ran to the bathroom. She put on her pajamas, made a simple dinner, turned on the television just in time for the 8:00pm round of sitcoms. She talked back to the television and laughed until 10:00pm.

Exhausted from her interrupted sleep from the previous morning, she fell into bed, but slept restlessly, dreaming about that ice cream truck again. Lying on a beach, somewhere, the ding ding singsong of the white ice cream truck crescendoed She looked up from her position on her beach towel. She wanted ice cream. The truck drove on top of the ocean waves that crashed to the shore. She jumped up and ran in the hot sand as fast as she could, and then reached the coolness of the water, but her feet slipped and slid in the water. She felt like she was trying to run through cold, thick, and slimy mud. The ice cream truck moved further and further away. She was breathing heavily and almost began to sob, but the ringing sound grew louder. She reached for the snooze bar on her alarm clock, dreamily, but the ringing continued. She picked up the phone, and once again heard the same voice, saying, "I love you." She answered, "Yes?" She heard the dial tone.

Cherylynn went to work the next morning and revised her list of people who could be calling, but her mind travelled back to the secret giving person that just wanted to spread love.

The next morning, at 4:00am, the ice cream truck took off into the air as she stretched her arms for its gleaming whiteness and the promise of a sweet cooling treat. She attempted to run up into the ethereal blueness, but could not seem to fly. She picked up the phone, and there was the voice again, "I love you." She replied, "Oh…," then heard the familiar dial tone, but continued …"I love you too."

"I'm awake now," she thought just a little perturbed at her mystery caller. "He doesn't give me a chance to respond, and he has been interrupting my sleep as well as my waking days with his continuous phone calls. Maybe he is a demon set out to drive me mad. Well, he's winning!" She sat up in bed with an idea. *69. "Yes. I can call him back!" She was hesitant at first, and then became bold. She pressed the "star", and then the number "6", and then the number "9", very slowly. She covered the mouth piece in case she lost her never to say what she burned to say. She longed to drip the words from her lips.

A woman picked up the phone, and said, sleepily, "Hello?" Cherylynn lingered with the thought, "A woman's voice. Not what I was expecting. I'm not sure what to say. Perhaps, I can be the one to give without wanting?" Cherylynn became filled with something wonderful; a feeling she must share, and she said, "I love you," then hung up the phone. She rested her head back on her pillow and smiled. She slept better than she had in years. A peace filled her soul, and she was eating ice cream, and there were no ice cream trucks anywhere.

She went through the next day at work with a certain grace. Her coworkers asked what she'd been up to: "Have you lost weight?", and "Is that a new outfit?" People who had never talked to her before, besides a grunt and sideways sneer, looked at her and asked her, politely, "Have you seen the mail yet?", and "Have you colored your hair?" When Tom, Shelly, and Carl asked her to leave her desk to go to lunch with them, she went. She had never gone to lunch before, and she laughed and had a great time. She couldn't remember the last time she had gone anywhere or done anything besides work. She left work when there were still a few other cars in the parking lot.

When she arrived at her apartment, she was filled with a certain excitement and anticipation, as if something was about to happen, or that she was supposed to be somewhere else, but she didn't know where. She paid her bills and balanced her checkbook, watered her plants, and called her mom to say, "Hi." She couldn't stay up all night. Tomorrow was another work day. She was tired from the mornings of interrupted sleep, and the long hours at work, but she was restless. She exercised until she was completely exhausted. Her cat, Sam, ran around the apartment, meowing as Cherylynn did sit ups and jumping jacks, seeming to say, "Mommy, what are you doing? It's time for television on the couch with me snuggled on your lap."

The ice cream truck tinkled. Cherylynn caught it, but they were out of rockets and missiles, so she had a fudge bar. The sound swelled. She picked up the phone, and said, "I love you," but the only reply was the dial tone as her alarm clock continued to buzz.

Grace

(Original Title was "Amazing Grace", and I had quoted part of a verse from the song in italics above the beginning of the story: "'Tis grace has brought me safe thus far, and grace will lead me home," but with editing and editing you read the story now where it landed in the end).

She walked amongst the lilies, silently breathing in the fragrance of the fresh spring day. The sun gently caressed her skin as she strolled through the park.

The young child had noticed the woman before. She looked like any other woman who had been walking through the park with her children, but the strange thing was that this woman was always alone. The lady had a graceful walk and an air of royalty about her. The young child noticed the wild creatures that pranced about the park would bow before her. Birds would sit on the lady's shoulder or fly around her head. As far as the young child could tell, the woman never said a word, but sometimes hummed songs quietly to herself. Occasionally, the woman would sit on a bench and just gaze about. She didn't seem to look at anything in particular, but rather she seemed to be absorbing everything intensely all at the same time.

The child had often wanted to approach the lady, but was too timid. Men would walk by the lady and some would even follow or try to speak to her, but she didn't seem to notice that they were there.

Sometimes, she brought a pen and strange book and would sit on the park bench

42

all day, writing something in the book. Every once in awhile, she would look up and smile at someone.

She had almost finished the story. Her story. The story of her life. She had been writing the words for years, but she knew she was still missing many pieces and needed to edit so many phrases. She wanted to finish the story more than she had wanted anything in her life. She was working on the final chapter, but still had some middle chapters to write. She was pushing the issue of ending it all.

The child with the freckled face, dusty brown hair, and bright blue eyes, who had been watching the woman, approached her and smiled sweetly. The lady smiled back. "Who are you?" The child asked, bravely. "I mean, the animals aren't afraid of you. They don't run from you. Are you a princess? The child whispered shyly.

The lady hadn't said a word to anyone in years. She did not know if her voice could answer the child's questions.

"Are you a fairy?" The small child asked, unencumbered by any teachings that would have stripped her of any open minded beliefs.

The woman hummed and tried to speak, but the words would not come.

"Are you an angel? Why are you always alone? Where are your children? Where is your husband? You are very pretty." The child continued, becoming bolder as she realized the woman was not going to hurt her.

The woman answered in the only way she could. She spoke to the child's mind, and hoped that it had not been clouded too much by this world not to hear her. "Who am I? Who are you? This is not such an easy question to answer. The animals love me because I am pure and real and walking with them. I am not a princess, nor a fairy. I walk alone because the path I chose in my life is a lonely path. My children are always with me and around me. I do not know that I am very pretty, but, thank you. I have no husband. I am not an angel, but hope to be one soon. Have you heard me? Do you understand what I have said?"

The child nodded. The woman continued since she had finally found a pure and receptive audience. "I come here every day to watch the children play and to be amongst nature. Every living being is my child; a child who I have adopted and have loved dearly as my own. I have grown frail and weary of the world of suffering and torments; of ignorance and pettiness. This is not all that exists here, but I have grown very tired, small child. Your name is Mara. How lovely. Mara. Perhaps we will talk another day like this. For now, your mother is watching and fearful for your safety. Why do I speak without moving my lips? Oh, child, we were all born this way, we just forget. I must finish my writing now. Thank you for stopping and visiting with me. Your mother is coming. Good-bye. I hope to see you again some day."

Mara turned and saw her mother approaching. Her mother said, "Mara, who are you talking to? A storm is coming. We better get home before we get caught in the rain." Mara turned to say good-bye to the soft lady, but she had vanished. Mara thought, "I feel sad now. The woman is gone, and I don't even know her name." The wind whispered back through the trees and the rustling of the grass, as the sun lit the spot on the green slatted bench where the lady had sat. Mara felt the rush of air hard against her ears; lips gently kissing the name, Grace.

Grace returned to her home on the fourteenth floor of New York's prestigious Builtmore Towers. Standing by her piano, she opened the lid and let her long, thin, and pale fingers lightly caress the keys; feeling the smoothness of the ivory and the warmth of songs played and yet to be played, calling from the waves of the lines of her finger prints. She tucked her long lacy brown dress under her legs as she slid on to the piano bench, placing her book, pen, and some wild flowers she had picked on top of the piano.

She inhaled deeply, closed her eyes, and readied her foot on the pedal. As she exhaled, her shoulders moved toward the piano, her foot gently pressed the pedal and her first note was played, as other notes joined in. Her hands glided across the keys, effortlessly, flying like feathers blowing in the wind across the sky. She played through the afternoon and into the night with her eyes closed until the rain and wind beat in rhythm with her Opus and opened her double doors of stained glass that led out to her garden patio.

The wind whipped her long golden brown hair about her powdery white face. A few strands strayed across her large thin nose and across her long eyelashes that began to flutter like butterfly wings flying home. The rain and sweat mingled on her brow and dripped on the black and white keys as she collapsed on the last chord.

Grace awoke the next morning with the bright kiss of the sun on her forehead. She peeled her cheek off the keys, which had made slanted imprints on her face. Her fingers were raw, and a few spots of dry blood clotted around her nails. Her scent was unpleasant, and her apartment was in disarray from the storm that had whipped through her life. Leaves were scattered across the parquet floor, chairs had been upended, pictures of the past were blown over, sheets of paper were stuck to walls, and a large puddle was on the floor where the glass french doors had flung open. She fixed herself a spot of tea and ran warm water over her hands to bring life back into them as she had done many mornings.

The clean-up took most of the early morning. She nibbled on a scone as she righted what had gone wrong. Her last act of the morning was to close the glass doors that led out to her small garden patio. She had a plum tree, lemon tree, a pyracantha bush, a red rose bush, and a small vegetable garden, which contained her two prized tomato plants. There was a small bench between the two trees and a sundial. She breathed deeply with the dawn, and the freshness of the air after the good, windy rain, when she notice a fragment standing behind the plum tree. Fragments, those shadow keepers and watchers of time. Fragments had no real substance except as a reflection or fleeting shadow. The fragments had found her again. As the sun cleared the horizon, dispelling the shadows in her small garden, the fragment disappeared and melted into the tree.

She had lived at her present address for three decades without the bother of them. They usually found her out every two years, but the fragments had given her some peace for longer than she could dream possible. She had moved from place to place throughout the centuries, and had found a way to elude the fragments without much movement or energy, but she was growing tired and did not have the will or desire to pick up her life again, even though, she knew she must.

She owned this flat, and wanted for very little here. Now, she would have to start over again…and soon, before the fragments were on her heels, wanting her story; wanting her life. She wasn't finished yet, but they wanted whatever magic or power they could grab from her. The fragment's numbers had diminished, but so had her kind. Damn them. They would suck the life out of her until they dissolved her soul; their sustenance; the fragment's reason for living.

Grace slammed the door and pulled the drapes in an effort to forget the visage of her nemesis. She grabbed her notebook, glided to the park, alighted on a bench, and began to write in her book:

"*In the Day of the Tribes, life was simpler. My memory is not as good as I would like in this area, but every day I remember more.*

The man stood in front of the cauldron as the steam puffed from the contents of sweet smelling bubbly. The man in the shiny indigo robes and sparkling conical hat made the cleansing gesture, breathing deeply, and bringing the smoky steam towards him, then up to the heavens with the full length of his arms. Peace filled his soul and the universe. The stars spoke to him about the breath of life; to breathe in the pure energy of creation, hold it, and then let it go to another soul. In these days, some call this love, for lack of a better description, but it is much more than this word.

We were ghosts to the Tribes. At first, the Tribes were frightened of us. We were so pale and white, and they were dark. We understood the spiritual gifts that connected us to the Creator, and how to reach out and travel amongst many planes of being. We knew the sciences and the arts and practiced everything through the breath of life.

We did not completely understand the physical nature of our environment, but once the Tribes were no longer afraid of us, we learned much from each other, but could never seem to master each other's domains fully.

We only came out at night because the sun was harsh on our skin, but we learned about salves to protect ourselves and ventured forth in daylight hours more often.

The Day of the Tribes was a magical time; full of wonder and purity of thought, word, and deed. All was one. Those who now remain have forgotten the magic that fills their blood. They ignore the magic when they begin to remember because the magic frightens them and seems alien, but the magic is the most natural of human gifts. I think the magic is not acceptable in this world now because it cannot be empirically proven; only known, but it will be back."

Grace rested her hand and her memories and looked through the life at the park. A chipmunk nestled against her feet, as a hummingbird alighted on her shoulder, and a small group of ants decided to crawl over the back of her hand in circles; a dance of a spiral expanding and contracting, hypnotically. She looked for the Mara child. She needed to leave, but wanted to say good-bye to the Mara child, and give her the energy and secret to continue the story of the life.

Grace had never been afraid before, but the fragments were too close, and she was tired. If she could not finish the tale, the fragment tracers would not get it, and she would have another finish her story, or at least keep it safe until she could return in another form. She would keep it safe with one that could hear her, no matter where she was, like the Mara child.

She looked around, as usual, but did not see the Mara child. A small child with a pale face, black hair, and bright blue eyes did approach her, did reach out to her with questions, but it was not the Mara child. "Who are you?" The large eyes of the child asked so freely and without hesitation. Grace spoke to the child, as she had spoken to the Mara child. "Your name is Sierra. What a curious name, but lovely at the same time. No, I am not anything you can name. Your mother approaches. I will talk with you another day."

"No. Not another day," answered a voice. "For your time may be the same tomorrow, or decades away from our tomorrow. Then the child is no longer open and free; no longer the child that can help you; no longer the child who can hear you; no longer the child who can save you. Don't disappear again. This message travels far from your Mara child, who is no more, but left this piece of her behind so you don't forget."

"Hello, my name is Mara North. I see you have met my daughter, Sierra. I apologize. She's still too young to know that staring is not polite. Somehow, you seem familiar. Have we met some place before?"

Grace could not speak, but she understood, and was saddened that her time clock was off, that her Mara child was all grown up, and could not hear her any longer. Sierra, feeling Grace's sadness reached for her hand to comfort her.

"Well, it was nice meeting you, but it looks lik a storm is coming. We should all get home. Hope to see you in the park another day, Miss," the old Mara said, remembering a certain kindness towards single women sitting alone on a park bench who could not speak, but only smile with large brown eyes.

50

"I can't lose time again. The fragments will get me. I can't hide in my flat any longer. I must face them and not lose any more time." Grace thought as she ran back to her flat to make arrangements for her next move; to tidy up old business. She would not stay in the apartment that night. She would run through the storm as she had done in her younger days, hoping to distract and confuse the fragments long enough to find a new hiding place close to the Sierra child in order not to lose her like she had lost he Mara. She would leap no more time.

After preparing for the move, she dressed in nylons, heels, and a gray suit to fit in with the others scampering about when they should be inside. She threw on a large cloak and decided she would run towards the park. The park had always been a safe haven from the fragments. They never lurked too close to where children played because the children could see the fragments and could warn others and cause a commotion. "The park, yes, the park would be my safest journey tonight. If I can only get there in time, if they don't catch me before I reach the inner sanctuary of the park." She grabbed her notebook and ran out the door into the growing shadows and the storm in all its strength, daring the fragments to come follow; to come retrieve the prize they had hunted her all her life to obtain.

As Grace ran from the nightmare that pursued her deeper into the darkness of the twilight, she dropped then stumbled upon the notebook; the treasure of ages. The edges were worn and dog-eared from centuries of reading, marking special passages, and filling the pages with blue ink. She grabbed the bound paper with her scraped and bleeding fingers and regained her feet and her flight into the night, which she had done several times during the chase. She wasn't as agile and spry as she once had been, but she was giving the fragments a run for their lives, as well as her own. The leafy branches of the trees swayed in the gusty winds, pushing shadowy pockets of deeper darkness across the landscape of the black night. Her lungs were burning from the strain of running, and her eyes wept with the stinging of the wind. She continued to run. She could hear her pursuer's breath in her ears, taunting her. Her dress was ripped; her nylons were torn and bloody. Sweat and rain dampened her hair and made her face glisten. She was numb to the cold stinging metallic pain.

Grace ran through the middle of the park in which stood the children's playground. Swings ominously swung in the swiftly moving air. All the playground equipment seemed to be moving as if ghostly children were playing in the violent night, and the fragment's sinister laughter echoed on the wings of the wind. At the edge of the playground were catacombs for the young to crawl in and get lost in. The mouth of the cement tunnels gave new meaning to the darkness that had consumed Grace's flight. Overcoming her fear, she ran to the tunnel opening and fell to her hands and knees, bumping her head on the top of the tunnel's cold; hard lip. She crawled for a while, dragging herself across the ground until she found a place she thought might be safe from her relentless trackers, and until she could no longer move. She gave in and let go.

Grace lay in the darkness of the tunnel singing a lullaby. The light had grabbed her, and she had woken in the warm spring air on a grassy hill, whose blades reached up to the sun. She sighed. The nightmare and the storm were over. She would return to continue the story.

The screams ripped through the early morning air. The dew was still wet on the grass in the park, and the gray mists of the early sunrise after the storm were just beginning to linger golden on the tips of the leaves of the trees. The screams repeated and ricocheted through the park. High pitched screams of terror with a catch in the throat of painful tears.

"She was sleeping blue, Mommy. Just sleeping blue." Sierra said, holding her mother's hand. Don't cry no more, Mommy. She wake up. She wake up now. Don't cry Mommy. We play quiet. WE not wake her."

"She is safe now, child. No one can hurt her anymore." Mara's salty tears spread across her pale; tired face.

The men in dark blue uniforms gently pulled Grace's lifeless form out of the tunnels on their hands and knees. Grace's pursuers were watching. The fragments had lost another one. They turned away and vanished into the wood of the trees before the light hit the ground. Sierra saw them out of the corner of her eye.

Tucked in her bright blue puffy jacket, Sierra protected a tattered brown leather notebook.

Blowing Kisses

Sam stood alone at the edge of the bar. She could feel vague images moving around her in the smoky darkness. Her friends had wandered off into the gloom of the dive to find the bathroom or to check out the crowd. Sam nursed her shot of Frangelico, mesmerized by the hum of the music and the glow of the indigo and white beams of light that lit the band on the stage. Another lonely hearts; lost souls avenue Terri had brought her to. Terri was sweet and well meaning, but Sam thought Terri had no clue of the shadows that lifted Sam's hand to her purse to pull out the cigarette and stare at the match's flame long after the cigarette had been lit.

She only smoked when she drank, and she only drank when Terri insisted she go to some joint and attempt to have a life outside the gym and her many jobs.

Sam coached the girls' volley ball and badminton teams at the local high school. When she wasn't coaching at the high school, she gave sailing lessons to over-the-hill married men, who always seemed to think she would coach them in their sexual lives, as well. The men quickly learned that the only games Sam played were sporting events that could be shown on EXPN, not the Playboy channel. Still, the men would take sailing lessons from her because she was the best in the area.

In her younger days, Sam had run marathons and won, climbed mountains, and kayaked down some of the roughest rivers in the world.

Now, she worked out every day at the gym, preparing for *something.* Her petite stature had fooled many as to her physical strength. She was a small ball of muscles created from years of trying to compete and hold her own against her brothers and to live up to her father's expectations. Her five feet two inches were never heightened by stiletto heels or platform shoes, yet she seemed taller than her actual height.

Sam brushed back her childhood memories with a wave her hand. She slid her fingers through her long black hair that reached her lower back and shown as ravens wings against her golden tanned skin. She loved sailing because she felt free, with the wind in her face, pushing back her hair and clearing her thoughts.

A voice snapped in her mind from the past: "Pull your head back in the car," her father would say in Japanese. "You are not a dog!" She would smile, her tight smile, and roll up the window of the car without a word. Her father would stop the car and make her sit between her brothers in the back seat so she would not be tempted to place her face out the window. Her hair was chopped short then, and without a woman's figure, she looked more like the boy Henry and Sally had wanted her to be.

She would stare at any light to take her mind away. When she was outdoors, she would catch the full moon, the stars, or a streetlamp at night, but during the day, the reflections of the sun off water or the dancing mirages on the road in front of her sufficed. Anything shiny would distract her just enough from the pain of sitting between her brothers in the back seat of the car as they barely gave her enough room to breathe and teased her incessantly. Indoors, she could stare at any light bulb or reflective piece of paper while her brothers talked about their many achievements and her parents listened attentively. Her favorite shiny pieces of paper were wrapped around chocolate kisses.

Sam sat on the barstool and pushed the memory away, then crushed the cigarette out in the ashtray. She asked the bartender for another drink; a "Flaming Rose." She watched the flickering heat of the exotic drink until the bartender blew the caressing warmth away. Like blowing a kiss…her father's hand to his lips, then showing her his hand absently as he read the paper, and her mother's pursing together of lips and pushing of air towards her as her mother stared at the T.V.

Her brothers, Peter and Andy, would run past her down the stairs and into the arms of Henry and Sally. Hugs and kisses all over. Lips to skin, not air. Smiles and laughter. The T.V. and paper forgotten for Peter and Andy as she smiled a tight smile and said nothing. When no one could see her, she would kiss the back of her hand.

At the corner edge of the bar, her eyes squinted as she reached for her purse for another cigarette.

"Hey, Princess," Terri approached. "Why aren't you dancing?" Terri was the only person who could make Sam really laugh.

"Men are afraid of Asian women, I told you. They never ask me to dance."

"I told you. They're afraid of your exotic beauty. You're bold with everything else in your life. Be bold! Ask *them*." Terri's smile was wide and infectious. Sam lit her cigarette. "Those things'll kill you. Hey maybe they are just afraid of lost Asian Princesses with amnesia." Terri's eyes went wide as she raised her eyebrows and smirked. Sam shook her head. Terri was strange.

Terri was one of those Anglo Americans who could never control her weight. She continued to jiggle long after she had stopped walking, but she wasn't fat or skinny. She had a curvaceous woman's figure, like Sophia Loren. On occasion, Terri attempted to define her shape by exercising at the gym. The first time Sam had met Terri, she was in the changing room, and Terri asked, "What are you doing here?" as if she knew Sam. "You should not be in a gym. You're already too beautiful and make life hard on us unnatural beauties."

"Maintaining," Sam had replied.

"No. You are out of place here. Huh! I know who you are! You're an Asian Princess. You just forgot. You should be back in your castle with Prince Charming, riding your white stallions through luscious gardens in a long gossamer gown. He's been looking all over for you, and here you are in this dismal place. Should I call him and let him know you've been discovered? Hmmm." She smiled and light seemed to spark off her eyes.

That was the first time Sam remembered laughing out loud; hysterically. Then Terri hugged her and walked away, leaving Sam standing alone in the changing room. Terri had instantly become Sam's only best friend in her entire life. Terri was a curious child; spontaneous, fun and one of those rare beauties that held the world in awe and experienced everything as if for the first time. Terri had asked her once, "How come you only *blow* kisses?" Sam's eyes had narrowed, her posture had stiffened, her mouth had become a straight line, and she had held her breath in; then relaxed everything into a tight smile, as if she had been struck and was trying to hold back a tide of screams.

The air and chatter in the bar seemed to grow thicker as Sam reflected on her life.

"Sam...oh, Sa a am. Houston to Sam. We are coming in for a landing. Okay, Steve, no more drinks for her. Sam...how many fingers am I holding up?"

"None."

"Okay. I think she's back. Where'd you go? I missed you. I was standing right here, and I missed you."

"I was thinking."

"You're always thinking behind those long lashes. You're always someplace else when you should be exactly where you are. Are you still planning your next adventure? Or are you just having flashbacks to a time that really doesn't matter anymore?"

59

"Another drink, Steve, and let's try to keep the alcohol in the same family. I don't want a hangover tomorrow. I have to get up early for a sailing lesson."

"It's Saturday night. You could cancel your sailing lesson for tomorrow, you know. You don't have to meet everybody's expectations…only mine," Terri giggled.

"Don't see you drinking much."

"I'm the designated driver. I have a limit."

"You're right. I don't have to teach my sailing lesson tomorrow. I could cancel, but I still don't want a hangover."

"Have you ever had a hangover?" Terri asked as she leaned on the bar.

"No. And I don't intend to start having them at this late date in my life. Steve, another Flaming Rose, please."

"Yes, Princess," he said with a wink.

"See. Even Steve knows you're a Princess in hiding."

"Terri, I've only had two drinks, but I'm feeling a little drunk. Have you ever blown kisses?"

"Yes. When I was a child, I remember leaving my grandfather's house. I didn't know that would be the last time I would see him. I didn't want to leave for some reason. I had hugged and kissed him, but as my mom was holding my hand and dragging me away, I turned and threw him a kiss with my hand and all my heart. I was only five or so, but I remember how he caught my air borne kiss and held it in his hand close to his heart. I wanted to run back to him, but we were

60

running late for something. Some adventure my mother thought was necessary for me to experience; ballet class or some such nonsense. I don't know if I really ever blew a kiss, but I remember throwing quite a few in my younger days. Children often do because they can't let go of where they've been. At least, that's what I think. Plus, real kisses from grizzled and slobbering old aunts aren't very pleasant for children. The aunts always pinched my cheeks too. It was easier to throw them a kiss. Why do you want to know?"

"I don't know. Just asking."

"What? Really?" Are you wondering if blowing a kiss is an unnatural thing to do?"

"I don't know. I don't want to talk about it anymore."

Michelle and Carolyn, the other lost souls Terri had gathered, snuck up on Terri and Sam and hugged them from behind.

"What are you guys talking about?" Michelle asked.

"Kisses," replied Terri.

"Chocolate or fleshed flavored?" Carolyn asked.

"Must be flesh flavored. They taste the best," said Michelle with a wry grin.

"No flavor at all." Sam said, squinting her eyes.

"Huh? No flavor? What kind of kiss is that?" Carolyn asked.

"Like kid kisses. Right? Like when a child blows you a kiss," said Michelle.

"Oh. I understand. Like the ones Sam gives." Carolyn said.

Sam squinted her eyes at the thought of
her own flavorless kisses. Her life was a tiny
silver wrapped package with no taste inside.
The band began to play her favorite song. She
wanted to dance, but she had no silver partner
of infinite taste who would show her how to
kiss a real kiss; a real touch. That would be an
adventure. That would really be *something*.

Sam decided to stand up and dance.
She hadn't danced since she was ten, but she
decided she wanted to move. She didn't care.
She was tired of being afraid. She didn't care if
anyone asked her, or if she had a partner.
Terri, Michelle, and Carolyn stood by the
bar in amazement at the ever silent and non-
expressive Sam, who found a dark corner of
the dance floor, and danced. Her usual
somber, serious, and bland expression
changed to an almost sensual spiritual glow of
intensity.
"She's finally here," said Terri.
"You knew she would be," replied
Michelle.
"Maybe for this one moment, she is, but
won't she just fade back into the piece of pain
she holds onto so very tightly?" Carolyn
asked.
"Never again in the same way. She has
opened the door. She will never be eclipsed
again," replied Terri. "Steve. A shot of
Tequila. I feel lucky tonight."

A beam of light struck Sam in the face.
Her dark corner of the dance floor was

exposed. The beating of the drum, the wailing of the saxophone, the boom boom boom of the bass guitar, the treble of the lead guitar, and the husky unwavering sound of the singer's voice danced with her.

A man walked up to her and asked if he could join her. She said, "Sure," not caring or even seeing him. All she could see was the music and light sifting through the air.

One song followed another, and Sam continued to sway until Terri tapped her on the shoulder, "Hey, Sam. Time to go. One A.M."

"The bar doesn't close until two. Can't we stay?"

"I've got to get you all back to your homes. We'll come again."

"It will never be the same."

"Everything is always different, but that doesn't make things less good. One A.M. is always our witching hour; our glass slipper hour. You usually can't wait to leave. What's so different this time?"

Sam hesitated and then said, "Me," very quietly, then more forceful as a sigh she had been holding in for some time which came out almost as a question or an answer she couldn't believe, "Me."

"Yes."

"Was that a test or something?" Sam asked.

"Let's go. There's a long road ahead of us tonight," said Terri, grabbing Sam's hand and dragging her off the dance floor. Sam turned to the man who had been dancing with her and saw him for the first time. She raised her hand to her mouth and threw him a kiss, then turned to the band, and threw each of them a kiss too.

      The next morning, Sam woke up in a fog. Someone was playing racquetball very loudly outside her window…no, inside her head. She wondered why the room was spinning. She dialed Mr. Robertson's number, but his message machine politely asked her to leave some words. "Mr. Robertson, this is Sam Ushino. I won't be able to meet you this morning for your sailing lesson today at the Marina. I'm not …feeling …well. I should be better by tomorrow if you would like to reschedule."

      Sam ran to her bathroom and heaved a mess into her toilet. She wiped her mouth and cleaned up the best she could, but the smell of the vomit presented a gag reflex that seemed to be unending, as she hugged the white porcelain. "Never again." She took a shower and sprayed some air freshener to lighten the odor. She dressed in gray sweat pants and a purple sweat top, only falling over occasionally against the wall when she lost her balance, which she found astounding since she had never fallen before.

      Sam went to her kitchen where she found a note from Terri. The outside of the envelope said, "Drink the hangover remedy that looks like tomato juice in your refrigerator and swallow the aspirin on the counter, and then drink plenty of water. After your head stops spinning, read the note inside." Same did as the instructions asked, then lay down on her sofa. She was feeling much better now.

She walked to the kitchen counter where she had left Terri's words and picked the envelope up to read the note inside. Just then, the phone rang.

"Hello."

"Hello, may I speak with Sam Ushino?"

"This is Sam."

"Sam! This is your brother, Andy. I was wondering if I could come visit you today. I'm in town and was hoping to see you. I know we were never very close, but I'd like that to change. I don't want to discuss it over the phone. Can I come over?"

"Oh, wow! Andy? I have missed you." Sam remembered Andy talking her out of running away and taking her to her Senior Prom when no one else would go with her. "We did have some good times, but there are a lot of painful memories too. Wow! It is like a ghost from my past calling me on the phone. How long has it been? Eighteen years or so? I just figured my family never really wanted me around in the first place. Why call now?"

"Honestly, we always cared, but we all had our own baggage to deal with from our childhood, and you did move around a lot. Dad even hired a private detective to look for you a few years ago. I know it doesn't sound like dad, but time changes many things. For a while there, we thought you didn't want to hear from us. Life wasn't easy for any of us growing up, but I know it was worse for you. Shoot, I've been seeing a psychologist. So, can I come over and see my little sister or is it too late?"

"I would like to see you. I always figured you didn't want to see me. Mom and Dad, I

could care less about. They never loved me."
Sam's voice caught in the words she had
always thought, but had never said out loud.

"Mom and Dad didn't know how to show
love. I've finally understood that after ten years
of therapy, and they are beginning to
understand some things themselves. I know
now that it wasn't their fault. When you are not
shown how to express something as a child,
such as, how to communicate and socialize
with others, you don't do it very well, and you
can't teach your own children how to either.
I'm trying to break free from that family legacy.
I would be ashamed to tell you about my failed
marriages and my two children who despised
me until a few years ago. But then again, I
want to tell you everything. Please, let me see
you." Andy began to cry.

"Are you telling me that I'm an aunt?
That is very cool. How did you find me,
anyway?"

"Dad's private detective called him two
days ago, and Dad called me. He was too
proud to call you himself. He thought it might
be best if I flew out to see you first. He wanted
me to test the waters first, to find out more
about how you felt, and if you might be willing
to have contact with the rest of the family,
some day."

"Oh. I don't mind seeing you, right now,
but it may take me some time to want to see
anyone else.

"Can I come over?"

"Sure."

Sam hung up the phone and opened
Terri's note:

"Sam,

Perhaps you will think I am even stranger for writing this note, but I see more of you than what you are willing to show. I know you have been carrying a great pain of injustice deep inside, behind a wall built carefully over time, for the purpose of never having to feel such pain again. You have kept those you would love from getting any closer than a blow of a kiss away because you are afraid they may be able to look over that wall. You built the wall to protect yourself and survive. Walls can be good that way, but the walls that you build for protection can end up being the prison of your true spirit. I saw you jump the wall last night, for just a moment. I will not be bothering you for a while with my constant prodding, but I want you to know that I am your friend and love you unconditionally. If you ever decide to take a few bricks down off the wall, and you need someone to make sure you don't fall or to hold your hand, or if you just feel like going dancing, I want you to know that I will be there for you. You just have to ask.

Always
Terri

P.S. And when he comes today, please, touch your lips to something other than your own hand."

Sam read, and then reread, the letter. Terri had always seemed to know the right words to say, and she would say anything to anyone, just like a child. She could tak and talk, but then become very silent and observant. Michelle and Carolyn had joked about Terri's intuitive nature and sixth sense, but Sam hadn't understood the jokes or Terri until now. Sam thought she had hid herself away so well, but Terri had always seemed to know just how she was feeling or thinking. Terri had known all along, and now she even knew that her brother was coming.

Sam's head began to throb with her realization of Terri's secret gift, and the thought of seeing her brother after all these years. She took some more aspirin and changed her clothes for her brother's arrival. Maybe she would take him to lunch at the Yacht Club.

Her life was changing. It was scary, but she had climbed Everest for goodness 'sakes. She had sailed around the world by herself. She was never afraid of an adventure. She was brave, but had never been as afraid in her life as she was now. It was easier to face death than life and being vulnerable.   Close up and personal with real kisses.

Now this was the real adventure; this was really *something*.

Occam's Razor

Planned Parenthood wasn't really around when my parents started their family. My older collegiate brother, Clay, was the first to bloom and surprise Mom and Dad five months after they were married. They claimed, to the relatives, that he was premature.

"Even when you think those child bearing years are over, and even when the doctor confirms your diagnosis, nature, the fates, and God, if you like, provide their own miracles and surprises to teach you a lesson." Mom imparted to the family before she announced that another child would be born to the Aldens. Miranda, the miracle baby, was born four years ago.

Mom isn't one of those stay at home moms. She had been a working woman long before she had thought of having a family and before she had met my Dad at a flower convention. Dad was a gardener and a carpenter by trade. They had glanced over some species of the Nelumbo genus, and my father had asked her on a date over the Peace roses.

*   *   *   *

I'm probably the only child my parents had planned. I have sympathy for all middle born children and second sons. I'm in my Junior year of High School and most of my friend's parents are way divorced by now. I should say, I'm almost a Senior and ready to leave the boring misery of my high school years behind me. Summer is coming upon my sleepy little village…okay…upwardly mobile suburb with a fast food joint on every corner.

I want to make movies; write scripts, direct, take them there move'n pitchers, work the lights, or produce. I want to be someone quietly standing behind the scenes, yet creative and powerful: wielding my pen over the actors and making them say what I want them to say, or pointing forcefully at the hired talent to show them where to stand, or looking through the camera's lens and catching the fading light of sunset in the tear of an actor's eye, or lighting a person in such a way that they look ten years younger or angelic or twenty pounds thinner, or supply the funds so everyone must follow my lead in all directions.

Summertime is upon us. My brother of much depth and the verbose speech, and the innocent newly forming sentences sister will have a chance to become better acquainted.

Summer, "the middle aged season", as my brother would say, will fly through the front door with the face of my brother carrying his bags, which he will drop, immediately, and find the first opportunity to grab me and give me a noogy.
*   *
        *   *

Just as I said, after dropping his bags and rubbing his fist against the top of my head, he says, "Have you looked into what colleges you want to go to? You should start submitting your applications now and get a head start. You should at least guess at a major if you don't know what you want to specialize in yet. Hey, butthead, are you listening? Are Mom and Dad home yet? I'm starving and have a lot of dirty laundry."

He has let go of his hold on me while he babbles, and I whip out my camera and take his picture. He begins to pose rubbing his chin or pointing or vogueing towards me as each snap sounds.

"Want to shoot some hoops in the driveway until Mom and Dad get home, Brynn?"

"One on one, or HORSE Clay?"

"HORSE. Help me carry my bags up to my room and sneak a snack with me first?"

Just as the whooshing sound of the behind the back from the foul line shot signals my doom in the game of HORSE, Mom and Dad pull up in the mini-van with Miranda, and bags of groceries for Clay and me to carry into the house.

When we're all in the kitchen helping to put away pounds of supplies Mom bought in preparation for Clay's homecoming, she begins to apologize. "Clay, I'm sorry. I know this is your first night home, and I was planning a big meal and all, but your father and I must go to a banquet tonight. I'd get out of it if I could, but the President of Getgo called me himself today and told me I had to be there. Well, the thing is…" she gets all weepy eyed and walks up to Clay and hugs him. Mom gets real emotional sometimes. She is a tough computer programming business lady who calls all the shots in her office, but she's just a regular old Mom-woman with her kids and Dad.

My Dad always intuitively takes over for her in moments like this…"Son, what your Mom is trying to say is that she really missed you and wishes she could be home tonight, but the situation is beyond her control. We weren't planning on going until she got the call from her boss today; consequently, we don't have a baby sitter for tonight. Can you two hang out tonight and babysit Miranda?"

"Dad, honestly, I was going to meet some friends at the diner at nine. What time were you guys planning on being home? Mom, you can let go now. Really. Stop looking at me that way."

"You've just become such a big man. You've grown so much in the past year. You cut your hair. I like it."

"Thanks, Mom. And I haven't grown an inch."

Very few things can embarrass my brother. Mom can get to him every time when she treats him like her big little first born boy.

Dad's always great at getting right back to the point. "I don't know when it will be over. We probably won't be home until around one in the morning or later. If your Mom gets an award…"

Mom interrupts, "The President often takes people on early morning cruises on his yacht if they win an award. Last time I received an award, he took us all on a balloon ride over his vineyards. We were gone all weekend. You were at a Scouting sleepover , and your Grandma stayed with Brynn…"

Dad breaks in, "We need you here, son."

I can't figure out why Dad is making such a big deal about the whole thing. I've taken care of Miranda many times. I even picked her up from daycare after I got my license. I don't need Clay around. He doesn't know how to take care of a child. He can't even do his own laundry, big college man…yeah right. "I can take care of her Dad," mumble grumble.

"Don't you have plans, hot shot? Friday night and no date?" Clay spits out thinking he's funny.

"Nope, Mr. Philosophy. I don't make plans. Speaking in Kungfuology you might understand: I float on the breeze to wherever destiny takes me, Grasshopper. Now, can you snatch the jelly bean from my hand?"

"Wise guy, eh?" Clay says throwing an orange at me like a fast pitched baseball.

Mom looks at my Dad. "Do you think leaving Miranda with Brynn is okay? If we're gone the entire weekend, Clay will be back…right?"

"I think they'll do just fine. We better get ready and on the road. Can you boys start now and finish putting away the groceries?"

"Sure thing, Dad." Jinx.

"Miranda needs a bath tonight and…"

"I know, Mom, she probably won't eat anything but peas, corn on the cob, or chocolate pudding with whipped cream, but we should try to get her to eat something else. Get going already or you're going to be late."

She smiles at me with this motherly knowing smile and rushes out the door after my father.

As Clay continues to put away the groceries, Miranda watches Clay from her peekaboo position behind one of my legs and says, "Who's he?"

"That…," I point,"…that is Grasshopper. Can you say 'Grasshopper'?"

"Graspopper? Not green?" Miranda says in her tiny tinkling voice.

Miranda grabs my leg, burying her face behind my knee. Clay looks over at us and says, "You shouldn't teach her such things. She'll grow up all messed up."

"Like me? Or like you?"

"No. Like those mindless beauty queens. Last time I remember her, she was still waddling around with a dump in her diaper, making goo goo gaa gaa noises and falling down on occasion…"

"Like most of your girlfriends, you mean?"

"Whatever. I'm just saying that she's like a little person now. We should be careful what we say. Hello young lady, my name is Clay. I'm your big brother; unlike your small brother."

I see that look in Clay's eye, and the hand moving in for another noogy, and I close my eyes, but nothing happens besides Clay wincing an "Ow!", and the sound of Miranda's voice saying, "Bad Clay. Bad Big Brother. Play nice."

When I open my eyes, Miranda is holding her fist towards Clay, and Clay is grabbing one of his knees.

"You've got some bodyguard there, little brother. What if I fix dinner while you entertain the little one?"

"You know how to cook?"

"Hey, I can fix a salad, and Mom had a frozen pizza here, and there is plenty of chocolate pudding."

*   *   *
          *

Miranda's favorite timely occupation is to go out in the backyard and find bugs for her terrarium. She really enjoys digging in the dirt and just getting dirty.

"Worms, wiggly worms."

"Yes, Miranda." I reply.

"Jesus loves worms too."

Even though none of my family are highly religious, the best and closest preschool in the area is the very expensive private Catholic Day Care Center a few blocks away. So, besides pushing the academics on the young minds, they also teach them religious dogma. I guess filling the young minds with religious stuff isn't so bad, but I always feel that young children shouldn't be confined by social teachings. Their minds are so open and free, but at least I know she's learned a sense of fair play from her teacher, Miss Crockle.

But, sometimes, she says things that really disturb me like, "I bad. I sinna."

"Why are you bad?" I ask.

"Mish Cwockle tol me so."

"What did you do?"

"Nothing. We all are bad. We all are sinna. But Jesus love us so we all okay. Jesus even love Big Brotha."

"You know you're not bad, right?"

"Lady Bug!"

*   *   *

Paper plates, plastic utensils, the tin of pizza, and a bowl of salad are sitting on the kitchen table as Miranda and I return from washing the soil off our hands from our bug hunt.

"You and Miranda want some soda?" Clay asks, standing by the fridge.

"I'll have some, but Miranda only drinks apple juice or water."

"I'll get it."

Miranda eats the lettuce from the salad, which is a real big thing for her to do. When she tries to eat the pizza, she does that thing where she chews the food a bit, then sticks out her tongue with the chewed food on it and makes the "AAugh, Aack, Aaaaah!" noise. I always grab a napkin and wipe the food off her tongue, and she always looks pleadingly at me, then says, "Peas?"

"You better boil some peas while you're up."

"She really doesn't like pizza?"

"No, but you should be honored, she actually ate part of the salad I gave her, and I must admit, I'm impressed with your salad myself. I didn't think you had domestic chores in your blood."

"She's changed so much. I'm reminded of what one of the minor philosophers wrote: 'Is the substance of life change? If nothing changes in life, then is this not death when change ceases to occur, or is death just another change in life?'"

"Yeah, very interesting." I make a "he's weird" face at Miranda, and she giggles.

"Clay brings a bowl of peas to the table with soda and apple juice. "A toast!" He says, pouring the respective liquids into paper cups, and then, raising his cup, says, "To change!" He pushes his cup against mine and Miranda's, and says, "clink, clink".

Miranda laughs and seems to be paying a great deal of attention to Clay as he expounds further on the theory of movement and change in the universe as he scoops peas on her plate.

She looks quite serious as if she actually understands what he is saying. Then she says, "Jesus loves Clay," with her eyebrows furrowed as if she is trying to convince our older brother of the seriousness of this statement.

"That is very interesting that you should say that Miranda. I wrote my term paper on a theologian who was obsessed with defining who or what exactly "God" was, because a small child asked him, innocently, where was God. The theologian answered, 'Everywhere.' The small child responded, 'Well, I can't find him, but when you see him, could you take a picture because my sister says God is a woman, but I don't believe her. I've seen paintings of God, but she showed me that they are all different. She's twelve, she says those are all pretend paintings. I need a picture.'"

"Brynn could take a picher."

"The theologian wrote in his journals, 'Is God what you give to get what you need to survive or what you want for pleasure?'"

"Pleasure," I answer.
"'Maybe God's the love that everyone on earth has put together; loving each other. Maybe that white light is all the love that was never used in life by all the peoples of the earth because they were afraid to use it.'"

"Are you afraid to use it?" I ask, taking another piece of pizza as Clay ignores my question and expounds further.

"'Maybe each one of us is only a small part of God, and everyone on earth put together is what God is.'"

I look at Miranda, and she gives me the "I'm an adorable little angel, and where's my chocolate pudding" smile, while Clay rambles on.

"'Is everything God that we see, or is there something out there we don't see that is also a part of God or is God? Or do I just think too much sometimes?'"

"I would have to agree with your last statement. For a family with no religious affiliations, we sure talk a blue streak about that stuff. Do you have some photographic memory, Clay? It was like you had to memorize all that stuff."

"It's not only memorizing the words of the great thinkers and their minor contemporaries, but also living, breathing, eating, and sleeping with the ideas. Since I was raised and am an agnostic, I find the theologians' philosophical works the most intriguing. I feel I am complete in everything in my life, but lack a spiritual connection which completes a well-defined and balanced human existence."

"How would you know? You're not human."

"Very funny, little man."

"What can you do with a major in Philosophy anyway? Become a Philosophy Professor or something? It all sounds so useless to me. A better topic would be how you are getting along with the babes at school."

"Pudding!" Miranda chimes in.

"I'll get you some, with whipped cream…right? The babes really like us sensitive deep thinking Philosophy Major Men. I get plenty of action."

"Alright, so maybe your major isn't totally lame. You seeing anyone serious?"

"I've decided not to even think about getting seriously involved with anyone until after I graduate. I've decided to complete a double major: Physics and Philosophy. You're right. There aren't too many jobs out there for Great Philosophers, but there are top notch corporations soliciting colleges for the best and brightest Physics students in Doctorate programs. What are you going to do with your life anyway, Mister Cynical?"

"I'm going to …"

"Take pictures the rest of your life. Yeah, the chicks dig that too, but you can't make money at it unless you're Ansel Adams, a wedding photographer, or one of those annoying paparazzi. Is that what you really want for your life?"

"I'm going to be majoring in Film, as in motion pictures…"

"Oh, big Hollywood man. I can just see it, your name in lights: Brynn Alden Presents…'I Was a Teenage Nerd'…or 'Raiders of the Lost Mind' …or …"

"Well, at least I'll get my message across in two hours or less instead of expounding on and on…"

"I don't talk that much…"

"Oh no. Just forever. At least I'll be entertaining people instead of making them fall asleep. I am going to be the best…"

"Butthead in the world! And many people find my philosophical meanderings quite enlightening and…"

"Stop. Your ego is blinding…"

"My ego? You probably just want to go into film to be center stage…"

"I've always been in the middle…"

"You're exasperating. You've only been in the middle for three years. I once met this undergrad who…"

"Clay, good peas and pudding." Miranda interrupts with pudding smeared all over her face.

"Looks like someone's bath time, and by the way, she is four; almost five," I comment.

"I really enjoyed our conversation. We will have to continue it sometime. I may be home late tonight, so don't worry. You've become a responsible smegmabrain while I've been away. I guess I'll have to stop giving you nooggies." Clay says, still in his pensive mood.

"You better kiss Miranda 'Ni ni' now, if you're not going to be here when I put her to bed. She won't sleep unless everyone who eats dinner with her kisses her goodnight or at least goodbye before leaving."

"Come here Miranda." Miranda runs to Clay, and he kisses her chocolate face. "Good pudding," he says and smacks his lips, then says, "Ni ni."

"Ni ni Clay." Miranda says as she runs to the stairs and begins disrobing.

"I better run after her. She loves taking a bath and is usually naked and throwing all her bath toys in the tub before I can get the water running. Drive safely."

"No, I think I'll drive dangerously."

"You should forget Philosophy and become a Stand Up Comedian, Shit-for brains."

Clay opens the door laughing, "By Butthead. Don't wait up for me," and closes the door firmly behind him.

*   *   *

I pick Miranda's clothes up off the carpet all the way up the stairs. She is standing outside the bath tub and throwing in the toys she wants to play with. I turn on the water, testing the temperature to verify it isn't too hot, then plunk her in the water. "Time to shampoo your hair." I say, following our bath time ritual. She wets her hair then says, "I want a dog. I want a dog! Why can't we have a dog?"

"Mom's allergic to dogs. Dogs make mom sick. That's why you can't have a dog."

"I want a dog!"

"Rinse." She ducks her head under the water as I rub the no-tears shampoo and conditioner from her hair. "Soap and clean, and then you can play awhile." I sit on the toilet opposite her and watch. They say that anyone can drown in an inch of water. Of all the things I do when watching Miranda, bath time scares me the most.

She is squeezing her rubber whale toy so water will come from the whales spout. "I want

84

to be a whale when I grow up." She moves her hand in the water, then looks at me, and says, "God is inbisible. How can he be? Water is inbisible. We can feel it." She splashes some water at me and laughs. "I get to go to the big school next year."

I wonder what Clay's Great Philosophers would say.

I think, most people look in the wrong places to find the answers because they think the answers must be difficult to obtain. I remember my brother talking about Occam's Razor. Occam said that the simplest answer is, statistically, the correct answer.

But, then again, there's what mom always says: "You can be and do anything you want if you really want to, but just when you think you're in control and know all the answers, the fates, God, or whatever, shakes your foundation and keeps life an interesting adventure, humbling us, in order that we know we are not gods, ourselves, sitting on Mount Olympus, in control of our own destinies and the destinies of others."

Perfection is also an illusion, I decide.

I dry Mrianda and help her into her jammies. I tuck her in, read her a story, and kiss her goodnight.

"When I wake up in the morning, can I have a dog?" Miranda says as she rolls over and hugs her pillow.

She's not waiting for an answer. She has already travelled to the Land of Dreams.

*   *   *

Mom phones from the banquet to make sure we are all safe as the usual intermittent Friday night emergency vehicle sirens play in the distance of downtown. I wonder if Clay is safe.

I can't decide on whether to develop some film in the basement, or to start looking over the college applications piled on my desk.

I pray to George Lucas for the answer.

Mommy Never Did Spit

Nanny Josephine told us never to spit, but Tom always found a way to do everything Nanny told us not to do. "It's most positively disgusting," Nanny would say, and Tom would get punished, but I, as Tom would say, was "apple-pie-goody-goody."

We played amongst the hedges and the luscious gardens of bright colors on the golden diaphanous afternoons of our youth in front of the large white mansion with yellow trim.

My mother would sit on the expansive porch, with its small spiral wood columns that held up the eaves, in her rocking chair; airing herself with her white feather fan that was intertwined with gold ribbon. I always thought she looked like a princess as she sat above us in her white lace gown and large-brimmed white sun hat, watching us dart in and out of the pathways as we played tag or hide-and-go-seek while she drank her lemonade.

On cooler days, she would dart in and out of the bushes, laughing hysterically as she chased us. Sometimes, she would kneel in the garden and plant roses of every color, but white and yellow were her favorites.

I remember running up to her one light summer day and hugging her hard as she knelt, digging in the dirt. "Child," she said in her lilting voice, "you startle me so." She smiled gently, and then wiped her gloved hand across her forehead to push a stray auburn curl from her brow, leaving behind a smudge trail of soil. Her bright green eyes glinted with gold, and she looked up towards the sun, and said, "Tara, my love, could you ask Nanny to bring me a glass of cool lemonade? The sun is mighty treacherous today." Her skin was so powdery pale and looked as soft as goose down. She always looked so fragile, like my dolls with porcelain hands and heads with cloth bodies.

Nanny Josephine lived in the small brick cottage behind our home. She was round and dark with rosy cheeks and always wore an apron and gave us fresh baked cookies. Nanny would tell us stories at bedtime and make sure we didn't get into too much trouble.

"Dang it, Tara," Tommy would say when I would win at checkers.

"Tommy, give me your hand for a whack. You know we don't abide cussing. It's not proper," Nanny would say with a concerned, yet perturbed, look on her face. She would sigh and say, "How many times must I correct you, young man?"

Daddy worked a lot and was disturbingly quiet. He was tall and lean with short dark hair, dark eyes, and a bushy mustache that tickled when he kissed you goodnight. Daddy would take Mommy out to gala events. They would get all dressed up for a ball, or the opera, or some grand social occasion. Once, on Christmas Eve, I snuck out of my room late at night to see if I could catch Santa Claus coming down the chimney. I didn't catch Santa, but I saw Daddy holding Mommy closely under the mistletoe, kissing her gently. I watched, for a time, while he danced her about in front of the marble fireplace, and they laughed, gracefully, with soft joy, while the flickering fire shadows twirled on the ceiling.

*   *   *

*   *

Our mother had been a preacher's daughter and had lost her mind a few years after Tommy was born. She would only sleep in the kitchen on the cold Formica floor; or sometimes on the table. The only time she slept in her room was during the day when she didn't feel well.

I remember coming home from school and running up the stairs to show my mother my good grades. Nanny stopped me as she shut the door to Mommy's room behind her. "Your mother is resting, child. You can talk to her later," but I never did.

Daddy never seemed much of much to me, but he gave Mom all he had, and Tommy loved Dad dearly with loads of chocolate face kisses. When I was ten, they sent my mother away. Daddy was all we had left, and Nanny Joe. Daddy mostly worked and watched television. We had one of the first color sets in our neighborhood, but Daddy insisted on watching the old black and white so Tommy and I could watch our shows on the color one.

*   *   *

*   *

One morning, after Mommy had left, Nanny was screaming and rushing us around. "Come now, come!" She shook me awake. Tommy was standing beside her holding her hand and rubbing his eyes. "What's the dang hurry, Nanny?" Tommy whispered in his tiny sleepy voice as he tugged on her hand. "No cussing, Mister Tom," Nanny said snapping her fingers across the back of his hand. "Miss Tara you get up, now!"

"Nanny Joe, what's happening?" I asked, twisting out of bed and into my slippers on the floor. For the first time, I noticed the gray lines in Nanny Josephine's dark hair.

"You are coming to stay in the cottage with me for a while." She hurried us past the room where Daddy often fell asleep in his big plush maroon chair with the television on. The room with the dark wood paneled walls with animal heads, a trophy case, a bar, and the gun case. Sometimes, Daddy would sit and clean his guns in that room as he hummed a tune he had heard on the radio. Daddy's study was full of strange people. "Don't look in there!" Nanny shouted as she pushed us past the room, down the hall, into the kitchen, and out the back door of the kitchen into the snowy morning like a wave in front of her ample body. We tromped the path to her home, watching our breath make smoke in the dawn air. She tucked us in her bed and rubbed our feet as she mumbled things I could barely hear. "Everything will be just fine. Don't you worry none. Nanny will take care of you. I'm the only family you have left. We'll be just fine. You'll see." She sobbed, every once in a while, and then continued mumbling. "The lawyer already talked to me. He said Mister Worthy left a will saying I would be the one to take care of you. I will be your guardian. You just don't worry."

I drifted off to sleep as she continued speaking to herself, quietly, as if she was singing or humming a song over and over again that lulled my mind to sleep. I think Nanny had been a gypsy in her younger days. She had purple scarves with tiny silver bells lining the edges, a crystal ball, and books on voodoo. She also had an altar to the Virgin Mary and crosses over her doors. She burnt many candles and crossed herself many times the next few days as strangers and policemen talked to her, and as we clung to her and pestered her with questions, which she seemed unable to answer. We all moved back into the Big House, and Nanny Joe would say over and over again, "Mary, give me strength to do what's right." She burnt sweet smelling herbs to "cleanse the air."

Tommy cried one night for Daddy. "Where's my Daddy, Nanny? I want my Daddy!" He screamed as she rocked him in her arms on his bed. I ran to his room when I heard him scream, and Nanny was there, holding him as I stood in the doorway. She held out her hand to me, and I ran to her side. Now, Tommy. Tara. Your Daddy is dead, and he's in heaven now." She rushed the words out as if they were too painful to vocalize fully. Tommy was just eight and still believed in Santa Claus. "You understand, Tommy?" I looked at him, seriously, and he shook his head, "no." "That means we'll never see Daddy again." I didn't cry because I was trying to be strong for Tommy.

"I don't believe you. I don't believe you! I won't listen to you. You are both liars! Daddy's taking me fishing tomorrow! You're just jealous! You are!" He put his hands over his ears and ran out of the room.

We hadn't been allowed to go to the funeral, but Nanny took us to the grave every Sunday to place flowers from the garden on top of the stone.

*   *   *   *   *

Until Tommy was fifteen, he waited and held onto a secret hope that Daddy would return to the Big House again, but he never did. "Nanny, I know I've been the cause of most of your headaches over the past seven years, but I know it wasn't your fault my father died." Tommy said to Nanny one Sunday at Daddy's grave.

"It wasn't you that caused my headaches, dear boy, but the night I rushed you away so you wouldn't see the mess your father had made of himself. I had gone into cover him with a blanket and found him that way."

*   *   *

*   *

When I was eighteen, Nanny Joe took me to see my mother. The doctors didn't think it would be good for us to visit her until we were of legal age and could make up our own minds about seeing her. She looked the same. Eight years had elapsed, and she looked just the same as the summer days hazy with sunshine. I felt ten years old again. Mother didn't know father was dead. So many years had passed, and no one had told her because they felt she wasn't ready to hear it. "Where's your father? I wore my new dress Josephine brought me yesterday just for him. He was supposed to visit me yesterday, but he never came. He'll have to take me to the opera for that faux pas. You, child, look wonderful. All grown up. How come it took so long to come visit?"

"Daddy's dead, Mom," I said to snap myself out of the trance. I wasn't going to be like her. I wasn't going to join her in her world. I was angry at her for still being alive, yet useless to us; for leaving us alone without her. Even though I knew she couldn't help herself or change what had happened, I wanted to hurt her as she had hurt me and Tommy; as she had hurt Daddy. I shouldn't have said it. She went to a corner and shrank down in to it and disappeared.

I went with Tommy to see her two years later, when he was eighteen, but she really hadn't left the corner. She looked at me like I was a stranger, but flirted with Tommy, shamelessly. "You are a mighty handsome man. You remind me of a beau I once had. Would you mind fetching me some lemonade, child, while I speak with this young man?" She wet herself as she spoke. The stain spread warmly across the white pants she was wearing. Her hair was tangled, and she smelled. She looked awful this time, and the golden glint was gone from her eyes. I left to get something to drink for all of us, and stopped to talk to the doctors on my way back. The doctors told me that she had been in the mental institution during the time when shock treatment was a common practice. They felt she would spend the rest of her days with them, and those days were numbered. She had rarely slept since I had put her in that corner by breaking her illusions with the truth.

I joined Tommy and Mother walking outside on the sanitarium grounds. It was a bright summer day. "Here's your lemonade," I said as Tommy gave me a strange look, and then turned and spit on the grass.

"Spitting is such a nasty habit and so ungentlemanly. You are much too handsome to spit. It ruins your mind, you know?" She sipped her lemonade and fanned herself with her hand.

"We must be going now," as I said this, her eyes looked at me so sadly, my heart broke.

"Tell your father to come visit, won't you?"

"Yes, I will," Tommy replied as he grabbed my hand, and we walked away. I turned for one last look, and she was waving to us. I could see the sun shining off the tears on her face.

"We mostly talked about Dad, as if he were still alive, once she realized I was her son," Tommy said as we waved back, and then walked out the gates.

*   *   *

*   *

Tom joined the Navy a few years ago and is going to be a technical engineer. Nanny Joe died last year. I'm married and have a five and eight year old of my own. I watch them run down the same garden paths of the Big House Tommy and I once had and remember my days of innocence.

The estate fell to Tom and I when we

were both of age, but Tom didn't want anything to do with the property. I maintain the Big House as an historical artistic community center. One room is my studio, full of canvases painted over the years, mostly of ghosts and dreams never realized, but some of the present, with the laughter of my children cascading through the water colors or oils. I'm living in Nanny's cottage, beyond the swimming pool, with my family. The kids love it here. My husband wants to move. He says it isn't normal. I cry, and we stay. I know we have to leave. I can hear the echoes of the past and my Mother's voice saying, "Nanny, would you please count the roses in the garden? I want to make sure none of them have died."

Chocolate Days

(Also written before the advent of high cell phone usage: Adult Content)

"Don't walk in here unless you have some chocolate," she says unbuttoning her blouse.

"Rough day?" I ask, rhetorically.

"Don't ask," she replies.

Her answer usually means that the rough day was worse than I can imagine, and it would be better to not bore me with the gory details. Her soft pink silk blouse falls to the floor in a lump. She begins to unhook her bra. I don't think she quite understands how this makes me feel, but the shedding of the blouse is always the biggest turn on. I only get that special feeling in my loins if she struggles with the bra hooks. The feeling I try to ignore the best I can. Especially on rough days like today. I hate rejection.

"Is Josh home yet?" She asks.

Our eighteen year old son, the pride and primary concern of his mother, has been scholastically challenged, but a supreme sports star, unlike me. We are both proud of his achievements, but she always seems to forget, being good at sports means practicing after school.

"No. His football practice should be over soon. He'll probably get a ride home with Coach Bud."

"Yes. And Alicia?" She asks, knowing full well our youngest offspring is the musician; more like me; very artistic. She's in the marching band and practicing after school as well.

"Her practice should be over soon too." I state.

"Could you give me a back rub?"

"Chocolate Ice Cream?" I query, as she slips out of her skirt and nylons. The nylon thing almost gets to me. She's so beautiful. I always wonder why she married me. She throws on a long t-shirt and some shorts.

"No, darling, all I want is you."
Surprised as I am by her reply, I think, "Why?"

She turns and answers my unspoken question, "I need my man."

That's done it. I'm over that edge of no return and try not to be too anxious as I approach the hour glass figure silhouetted by the burning sun filtering through the shades of our bedroom window.

I put my hand under her t-shirt and touch her supple breasts, finding the spots I know that make her lose her mind and become my girl. Her skin is so soft. My hands wander impulsively to her secret places as I pull down her shorts and underwear. She has already taken off my t-shirt and pants and is touching me where I lose control and become her guy. We both lose control and fall helplessly on the floor, heaving and touching, caressing and moaning, sucking and tasting, kissing and breathing hard.

I'm inside her and filling her with myself, my dreams, and my love. I close my eyes and see lights flashing as my body tingles to the unending pleasures of being one with her, then I can no longer contain myself, and explode inside her. We hear the phone ring, but ignore it. The caller does not leave a message. Lovely Sarah lies beneath me, smiling and touching my face, gently.

"Better than any chocolate." She smiles again, looking up at me.

"Sex?"

"No, you. Just you. You could have just held me, rubbed my back, hugged me, or held my hand. You could have said you loved me. You could have said anything that brought me back to you and away from the horrid work day today. I adore you, but you never seem to understand how much. When I'm filled with thoughts of my day or this or that, sometimes I can't see you. Sometimes, I get so lost, and need you to help me find my way. You always do."

"I love you too." Whenever I say this, she always changes the subject. I guess one of the reasons why we are together is because we both have a hard time accepting a compliment.

"I better get redressed and fix dinner. The kids will be home soon," she says standing up and slapping my naked butt.

"When you were asking about the kids before...you were hinting, weren't you?" I ask as she jumps into her clothes again.

"Anything to get your attention." She says, walking down the stairs, wiggling her fanny in a Marilyn Monroe fashion as I pull on my clothes and follow closely after her, acting like Groucho Marx.

"The secret word is Va Va Voom." I say, doing my best Groucho impression. She turns and replies in her best Marilyn sultry airy voice, "I don't know what you mean, Mister President." She giggles and scampers into the kitchen and begins the routine of deciding what to cook. She uncovers the basis for a meal.

I begin to help, and, every once in a while, circle my arms around her waist or nibble her ear. We don't often have time to share alone with each other. We always try to make the most of the time we do have the house to ourselves and aren't rushing somewhere or working on something. I make the salad. She cooks the pasta and makes the sauce almost from scratch, adding her own fresh herbs and vegetables to tomato paste.

Alicia walks through the front door, and shouts, "Smelllsa lika the sauce!" We laugh as she trudges upstairs to her room to put her horn and books away. She's a good student. She usually gets straight "A's", which are the bane of her brother's existence. We thought about having another child, but decided to adopt some kids in a year or two. No more babies, but kids that get too old for the system and no one seems to want.

The time passes and dinner is ready, but the door hasn't slammed open again with Josh's voice, shouting, "I'm home, where's dinner?"

I'm worried. We sit down and eat dinner without Josh. "How was school today Alicia?" I ask passing the garlic bread. Alicia, my daughter, with those large bright green eyes, like her mother's, responds with enthusiasm.

"Great! I signed up for Driver's Ed for next semester. You better start taking your ulcer meds now, Dad." She laughs at me. "And Mom…," Alicia begins, "Mr. Russo wants me to try playing the violin next semester. Could a violin be in the budget? I know, I know…I better get a regular job on the weekends or something, like Josh, especially, if I want a violin and to go play piano at the Salzburg Festival this summer with the Youth Orchestra."

"Your Father and I will discuss this after dinner and let you know, but money will be tighter this year with Josh graduating and heading off to college. Besides, you have the piano, saxophone, flute, French horn, and the guitar. I think the violin might have to wait for another year." She has a point, but I know we can borrow a violin from one of my friends, just like we borrowed the drum set last year. I know Alicia could be accepted at Julliard. She's that good. She's much better than her old man.

We finish dinner, and Alicia does the dishes; then heads upstairs to her bedroom to do her homework. Josh's empty plate sits on the dining table.

"I guess I'll fix him a plate and heat it up later. I'm sure he is just hanging out with his friends after practice." She says.

"He should've called." I respond.

"We'll give him a lecture when he gets home," she winks at me.

"Yeah, maybe he just stopped by Mrs. Ferguson's house to tend her garden." I say, relinquishing my anger and worry for a moment.

"He's going to be some landscape architect someday. He's so good with his hands and with plants. He can make anything grow," she smiles, proudly.

"Remember those tomato plants last year…and those roses? Well, he could be a pro football player too. Looks like he might get the full scholarship for football at State. I know you would like that." I praise him as she beams with delight.

I begin to pace the floor at 10:00pm. "Where is he?" I grumble.

"Boy! Is he going to catch hell when he gets home!" She says angrily, sitting on the couch swinging her crossed leg. At 10:30pm, anger turns to desperate worry. "Maybe we should call the hospitals; the police?" She says, teary eyed as I bring her an Eskimo Pie from the kitchen freezer.

"I could go out and look for him," I suggest.

"No, I'm sure he's okay." She replies, but means, "That's a good idea. Would you?" I'm supposed to be working on a new song for the band, and she's supposed to be analyzing some reports, but, mentally, we can't go to those places in our lives. I call the coach, but there is no answer. I call a few of his friends. I either get no answer or parent's telling me their son isn't home yet, as well. This should bring some peace to my mind, but a strange thought or feeling keeps nagging me. I begin to clean places in the kitchen that have never seen ammonia before. I move the fridge and begin to clean there too. She sits on the sofa, staring into space; clasping and unclasping her hands. Her brown hair floats gently over her shoulders. Not a touch of gray at her age, unlike my hair which is speckled with gray waves.

After cleaning every conceivable spot in the kitchen, I rest by her on the couch and hold her. I say, ever so gently, "Should I make a few more phone calls to see if I can track him down; then go look for him?" She only seems to have enough strength to nod "yes" and rest her head on my shoulder.

We both jump to our feet with the loud knocking at the door. "Something's happened," she blurts out and grabs my hand. We walk to the door together. I open the door tentatively.

Josh's football coach stands in front of us. Her eyes rest on the two gentlemen in blue standing behind Coach Bud.

"Can we come in?" Coach Bud asks. All three gentlemen enter as I help her to the couch. I sit with my arm around her as one of the officers begins to tell us, "Mr. and Mrs. Freejohn, your son, Josh, was in an accident tonight." She holds my hand with her nails biting my skin.

The three men tag team the night's events in consoling voices like story tellers, or a narrator of some TV cop show. It appears that Coach Bud was treating the team to dinner at a fast food joint after a late practice. A 31 year old white male entered the same fast food restaurant a few minutes later and proceeded to splay bullets into the crowd at the front counter. Twelve people were injured; three people died: one of the three was our son.

She looks at the officers and the coach, then me. "Josh?" She faintly sighs with disbelief.

I can't speak. I can't think. All that comes to mind is a silent scream. "My boy? My boy!" I blurt out, "Why?"

The older officer replies, "We can't seem to establish a motive. He wasn't a disgruntled employee. When we asked him, he just said that he felt like it."

"He's dead, my son, he's dead?" I question.

"Yes, Mr. Freejohn, he's dead. He died instantly. He felt no pain. I hate to ask you, but could you come down to the station to identify him, please?"

"Alicia." I say. Alicia who is well into her slumber, but looks…looked up to her brother so much. How to tell her? What to do? I feel like my heart has collapsed. My mind is numb, yet racing in a billion directions at the same time.

My wife collapses in my arms, weightless, as if the life has been sucked out of her.

The days following are a whirlwind of arrangements and sympathy givers. We don't have time to mourn. In three days, her hair has turned almost completely gray, and she looks old and withered. The sparkle in her eyes and the grace of her movement are gone. She walks in his room every night and sits on his bed, touching things in his room: the trophies, team photos, the packets of seeds, and his pillow.

Alicia forgets, and always sets a place for him at dinner, or waits for him to walk to school with her. At dinner, I turn and say, "Josh, pass me the…" or "Josh, can you take out the garbage tonight…" or Josh, what do you think about the 'Niners this year?"

None of us can seem to realize that he is gone. He was there and so alive one moment, and so quickly…so quickly, gone.

Sarah wakes up every morning and says, "I had a bad dream last night, Honey. I dreamt Bud and some policemen said Josh was shot and killed for no reason. That he was dead." She looks at me a moment, and realizes her nightmare was not just a dream. She begins to cry.

Every time she looks at me, she cries. Finally, I say, "Maybe I should leave. I remind you too much of him."

"I just miss him so much!" She screams.

"I miss him too, you know! You act like I don't miss him! I'm out of here! I can't stand this anymore!" I scream back from my grief, and she looks at me, stunned.

"Don't you understand why…," she begins softly, "…why I loved him so much. He was me and you together. A piece of you created from our love. I feel like we have lost part of us; part of you. He was like seeing you as a young boy. You looked so much alike. He had your smile. Please don't leave."

"I understand. Alicia is like that for me. I don't know what I'd do if we lost her too," I whisper, feeling ashamed.

Alicia has overheard everything and begins to sob outside our bedroom door, then appears in the doorway in her black jumpsuit that she has been wearing ever since we told her about Josh. She has a chocolate candy bar in one hand, and says, "I brought this for Mom. Chocolate always seems to help on bad days. At least, that was what Josh always said." We embrace her and each other and what we have left of our lives.

Court days follow. The deranged man who killed our Josh pleads guilty, shows no remorse, and receives consecutive life sentences in prison with no chance of parole. We are pleased. Josh didn't believe in the death penalty.

My question still lingers, "Why?" The man was found sane and didn't even attempt to fight against the charges, but was angry when he didn't receive the death penalty, like he wanted to die.

After sentencing, we go to the cemetery and place a flower, football, and a bar of chocolate on Josh's grave. He didn't want to die. We never thought we would lose him this way. The stone reads:

BELOVED SON & AWESOME BROTHER
WHO STOPPED TO SMELL THE ROSES
STRIVED FOR THE GOAL LINE
AND KNEW THE SWEETNESS OF LIFE

II
Epilogue 5:05pm
(The writing group I was with when I wrote this story in the 90's did not like how I had left the story. I believe they wanted a happier ending when I wanted them in tears, but for those who want to feel a little better, I wrote this to appease the group...)

The house seems so empty now. Alicia is in her first year of Juliard. Sarah, my wife, is not home from work yet. The "3:30 Blues" is the song I've been working on: the time and my mood. I always wait for the sound of the key in the door before I take the deep breath to smell her sweetness.

I miss Josh in times like this. After the hustle and bustle of the holidays are over: January; when the house feels emptier than any other time of the year. It's been two years since we lost Josh. My lovely Sarah dyes her hair that glowing auburn color and still manages the debits and credits of our county offices. She volunteers for our local gun control group in her free time.

But my music died the day Josh left me; us. She's strong, but I've been working on the "3:30 Blues" and the "January Sorrow" since he was taken.

His empty chair at the table haunts me. The unanswered phone call haunts me. The "Why?" echoes against my bones and is never answered. Trophies no longer shine on his shelves. They are tucked away in dusty boxes in the attic. His room has become a guest room, and Sarah's craft room.

The keys jingle in the door at 5:05pm. Maybe I should try to write "The 5:05pm Joy."

She walks into the studio with a cup of hot cocoa with the tiny marshmallows floating on the steaming surface. She places the mug down on the table behind me. She rubs my neck as I stare at the staff lines of my composition sheet. Three of four more black-dotted, long-stemmed notes are on the page since this morning. Progress is slow. She brings me the cocoa and rubs my neck even before she goes upstairs to remove her daily bondage of heels, nylons, suit, and bra.

I visited Josh's grave today. I spoke with him. I asked him to forgive me for blaming him. I asked him how I could ever let him go; how I could forget his laugh, his smile, his first steps, his first words, and that unique quirky masculine look that was Josh's alone. I don't want to forget, but I don't want them to haunt me anymore. I am stuck. I can't let go.

I turn to the table and sip the warm, sweet; brown fluid.

"Rough day?" My wife asks, touching my hand softly.

"January," I mumble, afraid to meet her eyes with my own gaze. Sometimes, the stinging pain that would bring tears to my eyes is too close. I don't want her to see. I want to be brave too.

"Come upstairs while I undress and tell me all about January." She takes my hand and gently coaxes me to our bedroom. She struggles with the bra hooks and stands naked before me with her arms wide open. I run to her, burying my face between her soft flowing breasts. The tears come as she strokes my thinning hair and removes my clothes.

Her softness still amazes me. Her taste and movement still thrill me. But I'm only halfway present in the moment. Somehow, I feel guilty. Somehow, I feel as if I don't deserve her.

We've had the conversation many times, but I can't seem to feel any differently.

For two years, I have poured myself into Alicia, and supported my wife's misery. I guess this is the first real chance I've had to mourn the loss of my son.

In Sarah's arms, I realize, life is for the living, and I am so blessed with a lovely talented daughter, and a beautiful loving wife.

The next day, I am inspired. I awake and write, from beginning to end, "The 5:05pm Joy."

(I think it is better without the Epilogue. What do you think?)